Four

Edmond Gagnon

Author of:

A Casual Traveler
Rat
Bloody Friday
Torch
Finding Hope
Border City Chronicles
All These Crooked Streets

www.edmondgagnon.com

1

2019

First Edition

Edited by Christine Hayton

Four

To all those who believe we are not alone in the universe...

Edmond Gagnon

Chapter One

I used a poker to stir the fire and feed it oxygen. Orange sparks set off into the inky sky like miniature Chinese lanterns on their way to dance with the stars. It was a perfect summer night in northern Michigan.

The distinctive sound of a beer can opening reminded me I wasn't alone in the world. My father took a sip and returned his gaze to the heavens. Stargazing was something we shared for as long as I could remember. The rustic cabin we rented in Petoskey lacked artificial lighting, making it an ideal place for our favourite pastime.

Dad stared into the darkness above him, as if conversing with someone up there. He was a man of few words, who spoke his mind. It's how he was brought up, and that trait he passed on to me. We never agreed on everything. Compromise was a big part of our relationship.

It started when I was the teenager who thought he knew everything. Dad said I knew nothing and I eventually learned he was right. I thought he'd be proud if I joined the military like he did, but he said he'd rather see me flipping burgers at McDonalds. We settled on a European adventure. It was his suggestion, and the best thing I ever did.

After my trip, I told him I'd applied to the marines before I left, but they rejected me because of a shoulder injury I suffered in a skiing accident. He did the grin and nod thing—his favourite response. Turned out he knew the recruiter. It seemed my father knew everyone and everything.

I examined his profile in the campfire light. I saw the resemblance every time I looked in the mirror. His forehead was larger because of the receding hair. He carried a spare tire but was still in better shape than most men his age. Stress lines stretched across his brow, ending in crow's feet that clawed at his temples.

Kevin Jordan was my father. I loved the man but couldn't remember ever telling him. We weren't affectionate that way. I told my mother once, when she was on her death bed. Some of my friends ended their phone conversations with 'love you,' but I felt it should be shown. To me, spending quality time with my old man was doing just that.

Life challenged my dad, but he did his best to be there for me. The war took him away while I was young, later it was grief when my mother died. He taught me to defend myself when bullied at school, and how to always be aware of my surroundings.

He never uttered a word of bad advice. He made a point to tell me he was proud when I got my degrees in architecture and graphic design, and always said I inherited the artistic abilities from my mother. We both missed her. She was taken way too soon.

Returning my attention to the stars, I slouched in my lawn chair and got comfortable. After locating the familiar constellations, I looked deeper into space and wondered what else was out there. Dad took me to the planetarium in Flint and I was blown away when I saw the moon up close. It really did look like Swiss cheese.

There was a gazillion more stars than I could see with my own eyes. It was awesome, and I wanted more, like the view from the Hubble Telescope probing deep into the universe.

What I thought was a shooting star caught my attention. It wasn't a satellite; the speed and trajectory were all wrong. Shiny and blue-white it looked like all the other stars, except it moved across the sky with a purpose. Until it stopped.

What the heck?

It changed direction. It went down, back the other way, and stopped. The object became brighter, as if getting closer. It flickered for a second and made a couple more manoeuvres. My mouth dropped open, but no words spilled out. I was about to turn to my dad and the object zipped back in the direction it came. It was gone in an instant.

"Dad, did you see that?"

No surprise there. He grinned and nodded his head, but it was more than a grin. He smiled. His eyes wide, his face taut, he seemed to be twenty years younger.

"What's the matter, T? You thought we were alone in the universe?"

I was to be named Tabitha or Timothy at birth, depending on my sex. Dad was a fan of the A Team, and his favorite character was Mr. T. He was quite happy to call me T. Mom hated the TV show and secretly wanted a girl, but I knew she loved me no matter what I was.

I didn't know how to answer his question. In all our years of stargazing, we'd never broached the topic. I considered the possibility of extraterrestrial life and kept an open mind to such things. Maybe I needed proof.

Is that what I just saw?

My father's stare begged an answer. "I uh…I don't know. I don't know what that was…a UFO?"

"You just answered your own question. You saw something in flight that you can't identify, an Unidentified Flying Object."

I gulped down half my beer, my heart thumped in my chest. "Do you think that's what it was?"

His eyes narrowed, and he paused searching for the right words.

"I guess it's time to have a father-son talk."

"If you mean sex, you're a bit late."

His deep belly laugh jiggled his mid-section. He finished his beer and reached in the cooler for another. He handed a can to me before taking one for himself.

"I'm glad to hear that. You know words don't come easy to me. I believe it's better to listen and learn, watch and yearn. Life teaches us lessons about humanity and inhumanity like the riots, my tour in Iraq, and the trip I took when your mother died."

I read how the riots burned and ripped the heart out of Detroit, and how the war damaged so many American men, but I knew better than to question my father on either topic. I was too young to notice how the first two events affected him, but I saw the change in his personality after he returned from the solo trip he took after my mother died. I thought his reasoning was selfish at the time, but later realized he accepted his fate, and was at peace with it.

"I understand the reasons for the riots and the war, but I am curious about the way you handled mom's death. I didn't understand at the time, I thought you abandoned me. In hindsight, I think learning to grieve on my own was a good thing. We all need to find our own way in times like that."

"I think you're right, son, but there is so much more I need to share with you. Being an only child, it's your birthright. It's time for me to pass the torch."

It was as if he punched me in the gut.

"You're scaring me. Are you sick or something?"

He glanced up to the sky again, and leaned forward, his elbows on his knees.

"I'm not going anywhere, but there are things you should know. Things that changed my life and gave me new perspective and purpose. I learned so much on that trip, about myself, and our ancestry. We have a long and important bloodline, and you are the last link in our family chain. Our forefathers were warriors, nobles and scholars, not just simple black folk who lived in the burbs."

I never heard my father talk like that before. I stared across the fire at him. Intrigued, I listened. I was confused by whatever it was I saw zipping across the sky. But Dad sat back in his chair; the smile hadn't left his face since the sighting.

"I know you're an intelligent guy, but there is so much you don't know…couldn't know. It's the way of our world today, we're fed information and misinformation by our government and the media every day. They decide what they think we should know and how we should live our lives. The government feeds the media bullshit all the time, our elected officials have been lying to us for years."

I found myself nodding as he spoke.

"I believe that part, dad, everyone knows politicians are liars."

"It's not just politicians, the military has a lot to do with it. Presidents since Kennedy have said they were going to get to the bottom of the UFO debate when they ran for office, but they don't respond once they're in power. Conspiracy theorists say that Kennedy was killed because of his interest in the UFO files."

"I've heard there's a book of secrets passed down from president to president."

Dad was quick to respond.

"Me too. I heard about it from a war buddy, who went on to work for the Secret Service. It does exist. Did you know more than one president has seen a UFO? Of course, they can't admit it when campaigning, because they would never get elected. Jimmy Carter was the most vocal. He openly talked about his sighting. Presidents since are more casual about the topic when asked. They make light or joke about it. Obama did just that when Jimmy Kimmel questioned him on the television show."

"So, what's the problem with telling the public and letting us know the truth?"

"You'd think it's the right thing to do but consider the consequences. People are afraid of the unknown. What if the aliens want to colonize our planet, or they're reptilian creatures we can't communicate with? Imagine the worldwide panic."

Four

"I hear you. Don't you think we have the right to decide for ourselves?"

Chapter Two

This story is about four men with diverse backgrounds, who were mysteriously drawn together. They shared experiences and discovered their common destinies and purpose in life. I respect and understand these men. They were all strangers to me, with the exception of my father. *In this narrative, I will explain the strange circumstances that bonded us all forever. To better understand each of the four men, the following is information I learned both before and after meeting them.*

The Italian

Devis Fiorido was a wealthy man, who would accept others as equals if they sought to better themselves personally instead of financially. Born of poor parents, he made his fortune in real estate. His estate and winery sat on the remnants of a five-hundred-year-old castle.

In school Devis loved math, history and geography. He devoured any reading material his mother brought home, including used National Geographic magazines that she borrowed from the doctor's office where she worked. His parents encouraged their son to visit his hometown of Torino; the home of many impressive Roman ruins.

Because of his excellent grades, The Italian was selected for a field trip to Rome. It would focus on the Roman ruins in around the Forum and Coliseum. Devis was enthralled by the Forum, with its haphazard structures and statuary, but disappointed by the ruined state of the glorious buildings that once housed the most powerful government in the world. Although he absorbed every fact about the Roman Empire the tour guide spewed, he was surprised by the lack of knowledge about his ancestors and their way of life. Many of the facts were based on theories or conjecture.

For the Italian, walking into the coliseum was a life-changing event. It was as if someone opened a door and he stepped back two thousand years in time. He froze on the concrete steps, gazed across the arena floor, and up the opposite end of the stadium to the open roof. In awe, he listened to the guide tell how gladiators entered through iron gates and ferocious animals popped up through trap doors in the dirt floor.

The Romans used underground canals to flood the coliseum so they could recreate naval battles. Tunnels connected cages for animals and quarters for gladiator slaves. Devis imagined the seats packed with people, cheering for violence and craving blood. The noise was deafening.

The Italian became interested in archaeology. His school principal put him in touch with an old friend involved in a dig at Pompeii. He was invited to join the excavation team in the land of Vesuvius. Devis studied the work of Giuseppe Firorelli, a pioneer in the field of archaeology. He established the technique of unearthing layer by layer, and in Pompeii he injected plaster into voids in the lava rock where human bodies had perished.

It was there, in the shadow of Mount Vesuvius, the Italian felt he was connected to the past and part of something bigger. He bumped into one of the plaster casts;

a small child appearing to reach out for its mother. Devis jumped as if he zapped by static electricity. Eyes wide open, he stared at the cast.

It appeared to be a little girl. He saw her face clearly. Her eyes revealed horror, as she watched her mother's body melted by hot ash. Devis was there. He couldn't believe what was happening and squeezed his eyes shut. When he opened them, he saw only the cold plaster cast. He kept the experience to himself.

The Italian became interested in stargazing. While contemplating the endless sky he learned the earth they dug up was only a tiny part of what lay above. The professor was impressed by Devis and took him under his wing. He helped him continue his education with government grants.

The result was a degree in archaeology and credit in astrology. Although fascinated with both fields, the Italian realized he needed to make money if he was to further his interests. He wanted to travel and explore other archaeological sites.

Joseph Fiorido agreed with his son that digging up old bones and counting stars would not put food on the table or keep a roof over his head. Devis told his father about the many tourists, who came to Italy to not only enjoy the beaches of the Mediterranean, but also to see places like Pompeii.

Devis mentioned a B & B where he stayed when he was in Sorrento. It was up for sale. His mother bragged how she could easily run such a place, and his father took the risk and bought it. The B & B became so popular it eventually became a group of small hotels and B & B's. Devis turned profits into land acquisitions.

The Cambodian

Harold Michael Carter was a Canadian, but he took a shine to Southeast Asia on his trips abroad and eventually settled in Phnom Penh, Cambodia. He was born in Stratford Ontario. The Expat who went by Michael, never talked much about his childhood. He barely knew his father, a World War Two veteran who died when he was young.

Michael dreamed of traveling and seeing the world and was afflicted with wanderlust at an early age. He set off backpacking across Europe and third world countries, while former classmates secured careers and started families. For him, a job was a means to an end; his next trip.

Carter yearned to get off the beaten path and go where there were fewer footprints in the sand. He sought out destinations that hadn't been discovered by the masses and aimed his sights on third world countries. They recently opened their doors to westerners, and his cash went further. He enjoyed places he could mingle with locals to absorb their culture.

The Canuck expat travelled light, had a good command of Spanish and got by with his limited French. He had no problem navigating countries in Central and South America. The only thing Michael hated about travelling was returning home.

His first foray into Southeast Asia landed him in Indonesia, where he made Jakarta home. It was a good base for his mini trips into Malaysia, Burma and the Philippines. Michael honed his writing skills and sent letters and email back home. He wrote travel pieces for local newspapers to make extra beer money. His travels always included a search for the best and cheapest mug of suds.

The Cambodian claimed a few weird experiences when he experimented with strange brews and drugs, but it wasn't until he visited Guatemala that he was really blown away. It was in the ancient Mayan city of Tikal, a place that flourished between 600 B.C. and 900 A.D., but for reasons unknown, vanished.

He climbed to the top of the tallest pyramid in the great plaza, the Jaguar Temple, losing count of how many stairs it took to ascend one hundred and fifty-four feet. Out of breath, and with sweat rolling down his cheeks, Michael admired the view of the other temples and surrounding landscape. He picked out several man-made structures swallowed by the jungle.

Michael explored other Mayan ruin sites in Mexico and Central America, always intrigued by the ancient culture that historians know so little about. He hoped to learn more about the Maya at Tikal.

He stepped back a few paces, turned and moved into the ceremonial chamber. The Cambodian examined the interior of the room. While staring at the rear wall, he focussed on what appeared to be ancient drawings or paintings. Michael took a moment to let his eyes adjust to the dark room. That's when things got weird.

His feet felt a vibration in the stone floor, beneath his shoes. A tingling feeling moved slowly up his legs and throughout his entire body. It was gentle and steady and nothing like an earthquake. Searching for the source of the vibration, Michael looked at the floor. A strange glow encompassed his feet. It turned bright white, with a hint of indigo. The light outlined his legs and torso and arms. Freaked out, he held his hands out and wondered if he was electrified, or perhaps, seeing his own aura.

The Cambodian spun around to look out into the daylight. He couldn't believe the sight before his eyes. It was as if he was standing outside, looking inside at himself. His entire body was surrounded with light.

Michael had a feeling of Deja-vu, as if he'd stood in that room before, centuries earlier. Images appeared in his mind, his body transformed into others similar in appearance, but of another time and era. There were flashbacks of the ruins around him, at a time when the ancient city was occupied and thriving.

A male voice called out and he snapped out of his trance. Another tourist had ascended the temple and stood near the doorway. The Cambodian staggered outside for fresh air. His legs wobbled and fearing he would fall to his death, he sat down to let his head clear and think about what had just happened.

The Spaniard

Like the Cambodian, Carlos Rivera was born in another country, but lived in Belize, on Caye Caulker. He was born and raised in Madrid, Spain, but left as soon as he was old enough, and migrated to the Costa del Sol, eventually settling in Torremolinos.

Carlos loved the ocean and beach and anything to do with either. He worked at a dive shop and got his scuba license. One day he took a cruise ship executive on a diving excursion and got offered a better job. It didn't take the Spaniard long to work his way up. He became the guy in charge of all aquatic activities on the ship.

Like the foreign women he bedded, the Spaniard couldn't decide where in the world to call home. He spent his youth with his grandmother in Jamaica when his mother went to Spain. He never knew his father. Carlos remembered strange things happening there. Grandma was the local healer and performed annual rituals on his birthday. She claimed he wasn't of this world.

The Spaniard became a thrill seeker and adrenaline junkie. His dive into the waters of the Bermuda Triangle was one he would never forget. He was diving with a buddy. They were separated by a group of Hammerhead sharks. His partner panicked, left him, and swam back to the boat. The Spaniard took shelter in a natural cave in the reef.

He saw hundreds of sharks when diving and knew it was rare for Hammerheads to attack humans unprovoked. It wasn't unusual for them to swim in groups during the day, but this group acted strangely, as if on the hunt. They circled the reef and Carlos wondered if they were hunting him. One of the sharks came close enough to poke in the eye. He looked to the surface, but there was no sign of his buddy. A large Hammerhead nudged the smaller shark aside, trying to be first to the dinner table.

The sea floor erupted and a sand cyclone swirled around him—a huge Rough Tail stingray at its center. The group of hunters were startled, and they retreated. The ray had to be six feet across and had no fear. Like a curtain of flesh, it draped itself across the mouth of the cave protecting Carlos from the advancing sharks.

He couldn't believe his eyes. The creature would normally have stayed hidden or fled from the hungry gang of killers. The Rough Tail lashed out at the Hammerheads with its spiny and venomous tail. One of the sharks got stung and swam off. Another attacked the Rough Tail directly, but the ray flipped sideways, and the shark slammed into the reef. Carlos reached out and knifed the predator for good measure. The injured fish swam away, leaving a blood trail.

The other sharks retreated, but continued swimming in a wide circle, seeking another avenue of attack. The Rough Tail did something strange, as if to coax Carlos from the cave. It positioned its body between him and the sharks, and flapped its fleshy wings, like it was waving him on to safety. The Spaniard saw his boat on the surface, a fair swim away, and considered his options.

Carlos took a chance. He slipped from the cave and ascended. The Hammerheads closed in. The Rough Tail performed another amazing feat and wrapped itself around him, like a living security blanket. The Spaniard imagined the animal as his mother's womb. He felt vulnerable, but safe. He followed his air bubbles to the surface. For a moment, he thought he saw his mother waving him on. She was surrounded by soft light. Carlos knew he wouldn't die. He was to serve a larger purpose in life.

He was nearly to the surface when a shark slammed into his protector. The ray lashed out with its tail. The sharks lost interest and moved on. The Rough Tail disappeared into the light above. Carlos broke the surface and saw his buddy Jake waving like a madman. He pulled the Spaniard into the boat.

Carlos yanked his mask off, peered down into the water, and asked his friend if he saw the Rough Tail. He told him how it wrapped itself around him and saved his life. Jake admitted seeing the Hammerheads circling him but didn't see a stingray.

The Spaniard asked if he saw the bright light. Jake claimed it was the sun reflecting off his mask. Carlos looked to the sky and saw two bright suns but wrote it off to blurred vision. He buried his face in his hands, rubbed his eyes, and ran his fingers through his wet hair. He felt odd, as if he'd been reborn and a new world awaited him.

The American

My father, Kevin Jordan, was born to a Baptist minister and his wife and raised in Detroit Michigan. He did everything a good Christian boy was supposed to. He went to church and school and got a job at a local hardware store at the age of ten.

It was at that store on Twelfth Street, in the long hot summer of 1967 that he learned how cruel men could be, killing each other over skin color during one of bloodiest race riots in the history of the United States.

It was with his father's guidance that he accepted that it was all part of the good Lord's plan. Kevin inherited his morals and was a patriot, who believed in God and country.

When the twin towers fell in New York, Kevin felt like many other Americans and believed the Muslim cowards were pure evil. He felt it his duty to fight back, so he took a leave from his job, joined the Marines, and fought in Iraq.

In that desolate and devastated country Kevin was reminded of the atrocities man was capable of, this time in the name of religion. His own faith waned, and it was impossible to believe his God had a master plan. War was chaos, death, and destruction.

His unit was sent to clear an apartment complex, a bombed out building in a decimated city. There was no enemy activity reported in the area and it was supposed to be an easy gig. Get in, secure it, and get out.

His Sergeant, Sonny, led them into a three-storey building. The entry and first two floors were a piece of cake. The third floor was empty too, but Kevin thought he saw movement outside an open window. That's when the exterior wall exploded and toppled down on them. Paulo and Freddy were with him and the Sergeant."

Freddy was a goner; a large chunk of concrete crushed his head. An RPG had blown the wall to pieces and they were caught in the rubble. His Sergeant called out, but Kevin couldn't see him for all the debris. There was movement about two feet from him, it was Sonny reaching out. He could tell by the company tattoo on his forearm.

A shot rang out and Sonny grunted. He was hit. Blood rushed down his arm and pooled on the floor near Kevin's leg. He turned to look out the hole in the wall but couldn't see anything from his position. There was movement in the rubble on his opposite side. It was Paulo. Another shot rang out and the bullet ricocheted off the wall behind them.

Kevin told Paulo not to move, but he still crawled toward Kevin who couldn't move because his right leg was stuck under a large piece of concrete. When he turned toward Paulo pain shot through his entire leg. A piece of rebar had pierced his thigh.

Another shot rang out, it narrowly missed Kevin's head and hit the wall beside him. Pieces of cement flew into his face and eyes. He blinked to clear his vision and saw a shadow in the building across the street. The sniper planned to pick them off one by one. Kevin worried about his wounded friends.

Paulo squirmed again so he reached out to calm him and a bullet tore into Kevin's left shoulder. The impact rolled him on his side and dislodged his leg at the same time. The pain was intense, but he used the momentum to roll under a large piece of the broken wall for protection. Another shot ricocheted off the floor between him and Paulo.

Kevin heard Paulo's shallow breathing, and it didn't sound good. He couldn't see him for all the debris and took stock of his own situation. The bullet passed right through his shoulder and wasn't bleeding as badly as his leg.

There was a space between Paulo and the wall and it looked like he might be able to crawl out of the kill room. Another bullet tore off the heel of his left boot. He had to get out or die there with his friends.

Kevin moved after the last shot and while the sniper reloaded. The space along the wall was tight and he had to push Paulo aside to get by. His comrade took the next bullet in the hip. It should have been Kevin's.

He heard a gunship; the unmistakable sound of air support. His unit missed their check-in, and the company was looking for them. He grabbed Paulo with his good arm and tried to pull him into the hallway as he inched along, but he was too weak. Kevin was nearly deafened by the thousands of rounds shredding the wall of the building across the street.

The American woke up in the hospital three days later. They told him Paulo lived, thanks to his efforts in pulling him to safety. It was complete bullshit.

While Jordan was unconscious, he envisioned his wife. She appeared troubled, waving him to her at first, but then holding a hand up, signalling him to stay. Kevin missed her dearly. She was in a white dress like the one she wore on their wedding day.

The American was confused. He wanted to join his wife, but something held him back, tugging and pulling him from behind. He turned and saw a long white tunnel with a brilliant light at the far end. His wife's love pulled him forward and away from that tunnel. A feeling of warmth swept over Kevin, his wife smiled and held out her hand. He grabbed hold and squeezed it tight.

When he opened his eyes, she was at his bedside in the military hospital, a doctor and nurse behind her. The American was alive.

Chapter Three

I sat there and considered our conversation about controversy and conspiracy. I felt connected to my dad on a whole new level. It was like the first time he took me to a Tiger ball game. I was in awe of the place. He shared his knowledge and love of the game. I craved a ballpark hot dog.

He tilted his head. "You want a hot dog?"

I didn't realize I said it out loud.

"I was thinking about the first time you took me to Tiger Stadium. I remember the place was huge and you let me eat all that junk food."

"I remember the good old days when the Tigers won ball games." He grinned. "If you go look, you might find hot dogs in the fridge."

It was as if the man could read my mind. My father stood up, put his palms in the small of his back and stretched. He picked up the poker, jostled a few burning logs around, and added another to the fire.

"You want another beer?"

"Sure, I'll get the hot dogs."

My dad glanced to the sky again and sat back down in his lawn chair. It creaked under his bulk.

When I returned to the fire, I skewered two dogs and handed one to dad. He wasn't the type of man who volunteered his personal feelings, but after our earlier conversation I thought I'd ask about the war.

"Hey, dad, I know you don't like to talk about it, but I've always been curious."

He took a big swallow of beer, exhaled hard enough to fan the fire.

"The war, I've never told you much about that, have I?"

"You've never told me anything about it. Mom said never to ask."

"Your mother, bless her soul, I told her some things when I was recovering in the Veterans hospital. She didn't handle it well. She loved everyone and hated any kind of violence. It almost ended our marriage when I signed up, but she knew how much I loved my country and how I wanted to defend it."

I leaned forward, my forearms on my knees, holding my beer in clasped hands. Absolute darkness surrounded us. Dad's face glowed like a jack-o-lantern in the campfire light. His eyes were locked on the flames but his thoughts were elsewhere.

"I've seen the scars on your shoulder and leg. Mom said you got a Purple Heart for your injuries and a Bronze Star for saving another soldier's life."

"A Purple Heart is a piece of medal they give you after your body's been mutilated by bullets or shrapnel. The Bronze Star was another chunk of steel I got for saving my own ass. Two of us survived that day, but the other guy didn't remember what happened."

Dad's gaze never veered from the fire.

"If you're a war hero, you should be proud."

He scoffed and crossed his feet in front of him.

"Haven't you heard the line? They say it in the movies all the time. The real heroes are the ones who don't come home. They made the ultimate sacrifice and got nothing but a flag-draped coffin and fancy funeral. Make it home alive and you get a medal. Make any sense to you?"

I didn't know what to say so I didn't say anything at all.

"You wanna know about your old man, He's a coward, not a war hero. Truth is I was scared shitless all the time. Going in I thought I was gonna get some payback for 911 and go kill me some ragheads. Truth is those men wanted pay back too, for hundreds of years of senseless killing all in the name of religion. That's the reason I stopped going to church with your mother. I felt like a hypocrite."

"I can't imagine what you went through, but I don't think you're a coward because you were scared. Wasn't everyone?"

"Not Sonny."

"Who?"

"My platoon sergeant, Sonny Morgan. He was a soldier through and through. He claimed he pissed napalm and bled marine green. I know better. I saw him die."

My father spoke, but it wasn't his voice. I heard a younger man, who appreciated the frailty of life. The wetness around his eyes glistened in the low light. He pulled his beer can up to his lips, but barely took a sip. I didn't notice my own tears until they rolled down my cheeks. I wiped my face with the back of my hand and took a swallow of beer to clear the lump in my throat.

Dad went silent, once again staring into the abyss above him, and maybe wishing upon a star. Searching the sky, I found my favourite, Alnilam. The middle star in Orion's Belt. I wished my father peace. He suffered enough during the war, and again watching my mother die. I thought about her.

"Do you believe in life after death, dad? Do you think mom's up there somewhere, watching over us?"

My father didn't respond. He dropped his chin and gazed at the fire, and then at me. I could tell he was thinking about his answer.

"Funny you should ask, son, I was just wondering the same thing. Your mother believed in heaven. I can't be certain there isn't such a place. I do know there's a lot more out there."

He slouched in his chair. I just nodded, offered a flat smile. He pretended to wave smoke from his eyes, but I saw he was crying. My chest tightened and my heart felt his pain. He truly loved her.

We sat in silence and I thought about my mother and the way she knew how to comfort me—like the time I got cut from the little league baseball team. One of the kids teased me and said I threw like a girl. Dad said he wasn't disappointed, but I knew he was. Mom said girls played baseball too, and not all boys went on to play in the major leagues. She told me I was special and pointed out how good I was at other things.

It was my mom who consoled me when I got dumped by my high school sweetheart. She tried to make me jealous by flirting with a football player and scolded me for not being man enough to fight for her. My mother said the girl didn't deserve me and assured me there would be others. There were.

I thought about my love life. A descent-looking grown man with a good job. I knew my dad wondered why I was still alone, but he never asked. It wasn't I didn't date or I didn't like women, but I had physical limitations that ultimately scared them away. Finding the perfect mate was never a priority for me. Family was important, and I felt obligated to watch out for my father after mother passed.

A satellite crossed the star-studded sky. We followed its path. Dad got up to stir the fire and stood with the poker at his side like a shepherd holding a staff. A burning piece of wood popped and scattered hot embers near our feet. We goo-goo eyed each other and laughed.

Chapter Four

The United States Customs and Border Protection Officer stuck his head out of the booth and his lungs filled with diesel fumes. Those who worked the line complained about the situation to their union, but they dismissed it as an unfortunate hazard of the job.

Traffic from Canada lined the Ambassador Bridge as far as he could see. The border crossing between Windsor and Detroit was always busy on weekends, especially on holidays like Independence Day.

The officer waved up the next car. A white Cadillac stopped at his booth. The driver and passenger handed over their passports, one Italian and the other Canadian. The man in the booth leaned forward to eye the vehicle's occupants and examined their passports.

He scanned the documents into his computer, asked their destination, and their reason for visiting the United States. The driver said they were visiting a friend in Petoskey, Michigan.

The officer asked how the men were acquainted and flipped through their passports while they answered the question. The officer took note of several stamps from foreign countries in both passports. Most of the ones in the Canadian document were from Southeast Asia.

It belonged to the passenger, Harold Michael Carter, born in Stratford Ontario. He explained he moved to Cambodia and produced documentation to prove his residency there. The driver was Devis Giuseppe Fiorido, of Turin Italy.

The officer scribbled notes on a pink pad of paper during the conversation. He tore off the top sheet, exited the booth, and slipped the paper under the windshield wiper.

He returned the passports and gave the men instructions on how to proceed and report to the Immigration office. Fiorido complied and pulled over as directed. Once there, other CBP officers directed the visitors inside and demanded they leave the keys and their mobile phones in the vehicle.

Inside the Immigration office, Fiorido and Carter were asked for their passports and subjected to the same questions they already answered at the booth. After more discussion about their reason for visiting the country, their documents were returned. They were told they could go.

When they returned to their car another officer said they searched the car and noted it was a rental. He wanted to know why they were carrying a box of road flares. They were not part of an emergency kit. Fiorido said he wasn't sure he could bring fireworks over the border and the flares were to light the beach at his friend's cottage.

The CBP Officer looked to his female partner and she shrugged. He closed the trunk and nodded. They were free to leave. The Italian man reached into the console for a pack of cigarettes, lit one and took a long pull. He blew a stream of smoke out the open window.

Carter had only seen his friend smoke when they drank. Fiorido acknowledged the look and said he needed a cocktail. He felt like they were interrogated by the Gestapo. Carter nodded in agreement and said it's been like that ever since 911. He used to cross the border all the time with his cop buddy from Windsor. Back then his friend just flashed his badge and got waved through.

Ten minutes later the front line CBP Officer was relieved from his post. It wasn't his scheduled break and he was puzzled. His replacement told him to report to the supervisor. He stepped into the boss's office and was confronted by two men in dark suits. They questioned him about the two foreigners in the rented Cadillac and asked him things he'd already documented.

The military-looking men were particularly interested in the foreigners' destination, why they were going there, and who they were visiting. With their questions answered, they left without explaining their inquiry. The officer asked his boss who the two men were. He explained they produced FBI badges, and he shouldn't worry about it.

About an hour later, a black SUV exited Interstate Highway 75 North and pulled into a shopping mall parking lot. The passenger took a cursory glance at the driver but no explanation was needed. It was understood they would change their wardrobe to better blend with the cottage crowd in Northern Michigan. They went shopping.

With new attire in hand, they opened the back hatch of the SUV and removed their black suit coats, and ties. They unclipped the guns and badges from their belts. The tin shields read *Federal Investigations Bureau*. The identification bore an uncanny resemblance to badges worn by the FBI.

Chapter Five

The inside of the refrigerator in the cottage resembled mine at home: mostly empty. Eyeing leftover pizza, I grabbed a slice and shoved it in my mouth. The top shelf was loaded with beer. I knocked three cans to the floor when I reached in for the hot dogs. Chuckling to myself, I took note of the dented can to make sure dad got that one.

After loading a serving tray with condiments, I devoured the last of the pizza—no use leaving one piece in the fridge all by itself. Dogs, buns, mustard, ketchup, chopped onions for dad and mayo for me. Everything we needed for gourmet hotdogs.

Shit. Cheese! Gotta have cheese...and bacon...no, that's too much work and I might burn the place down.

It was a nice little cottage. My parents rented it for their honeymoon. It was a serene place and dad and I returned annually for Independence Day, which was also his birthday. The cottage belonged to a cousin on my mother's side of the family. They owned property in Petoskey and nearby Harbour Springs. The land alone was worth a fortune because of its location on Lake Michigan.

Although in disrepair, it served our purpose. Dad always travelled with a toolbox and enjoyed puttering. He made small repairs during our stay. He couldn't afford to buy the place and thought fixing it up might keep the owners from selling it.

I picked up the tray and almost made it to the back door. *Doritos!* With the nacho chips in hand I closed the cupboard. I thought I saw headlights in the driveway. We weren't expecting company, and I wrote it off to someone visiting one of the neighbouring cottages. At the back door I paused and wondered what I'd forgotten. *Pee!* The hunt for munchies got me sidetracked and I forgot to relieve myself.

My reflection stared back at me from the mirror. Like most men I knew, I wished for a bigger penis. Maybe that was my problem with women, did they really think bigger was better? My hazel eyes were my mother's, the double chin and high forehead, my father's. After a tug and a shake, I patted myself on the stomach, glad I didn't have my dad's paunch—not yet anyway.

Admiring myself for a few more seconds, I remembered one of my friends trying to get us into a bar by saying I was Denzel Washington. In a dark room with a blind doorman…maybe.

I took a final inventory of everything in hand. I heard voices by the campfire. When I rounded the corner, I saw two figures. One on either side of my father. The light from the fire revealed the features of two men. One was European and the other white. They greeted me when I stepped into their circle.

"Great, a weenie roast!" Cracked the white guy who gawked at the loaded serving tray.

My gaze stayed on my father standing in the middle with one arm around each man's shoulder.

"Son, this is Michael and Devis, better known as the Cambodian and the Italian."

Two hands shot forward to seal the introductions. I shook the Italian's first, then the Cambodian's.

"Just call me T, my dad does."

The quick-witted Cambodian eyed me.

"Mister T, eh? Your father mentioned he was a big fan of the A-Team. I liked Murdoch, the crazy one."

Dad responded, "Careful, Michael, your Canuck roots are showing…eh?"

My father and I laughed. The Italian didn't get the joke.

The Cambodian defended himself.

"It's a bad habit that surfaces whenever I visit family across the border. My niece and her husband live in Windsor. He's a cop there and he took me for a ride-a-long the other night. It started out quiet, but there were two shootings."

Dad scoffed and slapped him on the shoulder.

"Shit, that's an hourly occurrence in Detroit."

The Italian thought that was funny.

"T, get our guests a couple of chairs from the shed."

He popped the cooler open and reached in for beer.

"And more Bud Light…I thought that's why you went inside?"

Beer. That's the other reason I went into the cottage.

I fetched the chairs, and made a beer run. I opened the fridge and cracked a smile, I had to make sure dad got the can that fell on the floor. I snickered and headed back to the fire. The three men stood together, slapping each other on the back, and laughing. When I rounded the fire and reached for the cooler, I thought I saw a faint yellow glow hanging over them. *Must be my beer buzz,* I shrugged it off.

I plopped a dozen cans into the cooler, checked them carefully to find the dented one, and handed each man a beer. Dad said he wanted to make a toast and he popped the top of his can. A foamy geyser shot up the front of his shirt, hit him under the chin, and went airborne when he aimed it at the fire.

The flames hissed back at him, and laughter erupted. My father briefly gave me the stink-eye. He always appreciated a good gag and joined in. He put his mouth on the overflowing can and slurped the beer. He raised it up and offered a toast.

"To our birthday!"

We all raised our cans and repeated, "To our birthday."

I wondered why everyone said it was *our* birthday.

The Italian joined the conversation and spoke up.

"This is a nice little place you have up here in the middle of nowhere—looks perfect for stargazing."

"You wanna buy it, Devis? It's for sale."

"What? Why would you sell such a beautiful property?"

"Because I don't own it, my rich friend. So, do you wanna buy it? We'll rent it from you. T and I come here every year."

The Italian chewed on the idea for a moment.

"Maybe, I don't own anything in America...yet."

He pulled out his cigarettes and lit one up.

The Cambodian chortled.

"There you go, Devis, it could be a good place for a Bed & Breakfast but you'd have to serve American the style here with bacon and eggs, not your buns and jelly continental style."

I noticed how comfortable the men were with each other, how the three of them poked fun and carried on like they were brothers. I worked a hot dog onto a metal skewer. The old guys talked among themselves.

I asked my dad, "Where's the other one, the guy you call the Spaniard?"

Their mouths stopped moving and the two foreigners eyed my father. He lifted his chin and considered me.

"We're not sure, son, we haven't seen him since Egypt. That was our last birthday when we agreed to make this an annual thing. I really didn't think anyone would show up."

The Cambodian chimed in.

"How could we miss our birthday?"

Obviously not shy, he helped himself to another beer. Maybe my hearing was going. Why did they keep saying *our* birthday?

The three of them gazed skyward, my dad doing his smile and nod thing. I noticed my wiener was burning and yanked it from the fire.

"Anyone else want a hot dog?"

Nobody answered. The three amigos were engaged in their own conversation. I grabbed a fistful of Doritos, shoved them in my mouth, and returned my meat to the fire.

Chapter Six

The Italian broke from the threesome to fetch himself a beer. He popped the top of the can and looked me over like a piece of real estate he was considering. Self-conscious, I worried about gobs of mustard or mayo on my face. I wiped the corners of my mouth with the back of my hand. I loved mayonnaise and put that shit on everything.

The Italian pulled his chair next to mine and sat down.

"Your father tells me you travelled in Europe."

Content the junk food I consumed soaked up some of the alcohol in my stomach and I could speak coherently, I nodded. I noted his Italian accent for the first time.

"Two months in Western Europe. I flew into London but overbooking and flight delays cut my time there to only a couple of rushed days. I experienced the city from the back seat of a taxi. It was one of those old-fashioned black ones. The sympathetic driver took me on a kamikaze tour of the major sites.

"I took a train to Dover and crossed the English Channel by ferry during a really bad storm. It was scary. Tables of food and drinks toppled over and people were sick everywhere. Some stood outside in the rain and puked over the railing. I braced myself in a corner on a bench so I didn't fall over. Going to the bathroom was like riding a roller coaster.

"The rain continued as I entered France but let up during the train ride to Paris. I stopped at the first café I saw and learned a beer cost as much as my train ticket. That expensive lesson taught me to watch where the locals went."

The Italian nodded along and seemed genuinely interested in my babbling travelogue so I continued.

"I did the usual sites like the Eiffel Tower, Notre Dame, Arch de Triumph, and a quick tour of the Louver just to see the Mona Lisa and say I'd been there. The place was huge and I didn't want to spend a whole week in one museum.

"The Palace of Versailles was amazing, but after seeing such extravagance, I understood why the French people revolted and beheaded their royals."

Devis shifted in his chair, took a pull off his can of beer.

"And what did you think about the French people?"

I didn't know why he was asking, but I answered honestly.

"They were pretty rude, actually. I met a Canadian girl in the Latin Quarter. She explained how the French don't like Americans and gave me a maple leaf flag to pin on my backpack."

"Ah, yes, it seems after the war you Americanos left many in Europe with...what do you say...a bad flavor in their mouth? Some Italians feel the same way, but if it wasn't for your countrymen and your allies Rome would serve beer and bratwurst, and I would speak German."

I offered him some Doritos; he shook his head.

"I guess I understand. When I lied and told people I was Canadian, they treated me completely different."

He smiled and nodded.

"Did you visit my homeland, Italy?"

"I used my rail pass to get to Venice. It was truly amazing and the most unique place I ever visited. I crossed overland to Cinque Terre; five little villages perched on cliffs overlooking the Mediterranean."

"Yes, yes…I know the area well. Riomaggiore is my home now, do you remember the town?"

I rubbed my chin in thought. The trip happened a few years earlier, but it was a blur in my mind. Probably had something to do with that coffee house in Holland.

"Honestly, Devis, I enjoyed the area immensely, but I don't remember the individual villages. They were all great. In one place I watched the sunset from the top of an old castle overlooking the marina. All the different coloured fishing boats were cool. They told me it was so wives could identify their husbands coming home from sea."

"Vernazza. Like the others, it was a fishing village before the whole area became a tourist hot spot. It is beautiful."

"I continued south to Rome, where I was most impressed by the coliseum."

I tried in vain to get more Doritos into my mouth, but I was doing all the talking and didn't want to spew pieces all over my dad's guest. I offered the bag to the Italian but he shook his head.

"Thank you, no, but I would like to try one of your American wiener dogs."

He flicked his cigarette butt into the fire. I got up to grab him a skewer and hot dog. The Italian continued, while I prepped his meat.

"I loved the coliseum too. I saw it for the first time when I was in school."

"When I stood inside the arena, I felt like I'd been there before, in another life or something. It was weird."

I handed the skewer to him, tilted my head towards the fire. He thrust it into the flames and looked to me for approval.

"Amazing. That's exactly how I felt when I visited Rome the first time. Maybe we were both there before, in another life." The Italian smiled and winked.

I snorted. "Whatever. I was blown away by Pompeii too. It was like visiting a giant graveyard."

The Italian chuckled. "Some called me the grave digger, when I worked an archaeological site there as a student."

"Wow that must have been cool."

I rotated my hand and showed him how to turn his hot dog so it wouldn't burn. He juggled the skewer, his cigarette, and his beer can to complete the manoeuvre. The butt bobbed up and down in the corner of his mouth when he spoke, and he had to squint to keep smoke from his eyes.

"It was very hot and very hard work, but yes, really cool. Did you visit Sorrento?"

"Yes, but for only a short stay. I wanted to spend more time on the beach there, but I couldn't find long term lodging. I had to shack up with two girls from L.A. and a guy from Sweden. We shared a suite none of us could have afforded on our own. It was a beautiful place with a huge patio overlooking the Mediterranean with the beaches down below."

His dark eyes widened and reflected the campfire light.

"Do you remember the name of the place you stayed in?"

"I dunno...a villa or something...Polo or Paulo maybe."

The Italian jumped from his chair and knocked over the beer at his feet. He threw his arms up with the hot dog in one hand, and his smoke in the other.

He shouted, "Villa Pula!"

A swallow of beer slipped down my windpipe and choked me. I coughed my words when I attempted an answer.

"Yeah, that could be it. An old couple ran the place."

The Italian casually flicked his butt at the fire, smacked himself on the forehead with an open palm, and sat down. My father and Michael glanced our way but continued their private conversation. Devis shook his head.

"The old couple you met are my parents. The place where you stayed is their Bed & Breakfast. It's the one that started it all, they named it after the town of their birth. Mama Mia, I can't believe you stayed there."

He caught himself, noticing how excited he was.

"I'm sorry. This is your story. Please go on."

I took a drink of beer, my throat still rough as though I swallowed sand.

"After Sorrento I took the train to Brindisi, and then the ferry to Greece."

The conversation on the other side of the campfire stopped. The Cambodian popped another beer can and shook his head.

"Please, don't get him going on about Greece."

Chapter Seven

I remembered most of Greece, certain parts more than others. Devis enjoyed his hot dog while he listened. A gob of mustard fell from the end of his bun and narrowly missed one of his expensive loafers.

"My ferry dropped passengers in Corfu, but I stayed on until Athens and roomed in the Plaka, under the shadow of the Acropolis. I climbed to the top and thought it was no big deal, until I sat on the steps amongst those giant marble columns. They have stood as sentinels for over two thousand years.

"A wave of emotion washed over me. Greek legends from ancient civilizations stood right where I sat. Wars were fought and bombs exploded there. The towering pillars remained; symbols of a lost era."

The man from Italy jawed the last bite of his frankfurter. I shifted my gaze from him to the fire and spilled the truth of what I'd come to believe.

"I don't think I'm the only one it's happened to, but once again I felt like I'd been there before." I chuckled. "Maybe I'm a descendant of Alexander the Great."

My dad and the Cambodian stopped talking and gawked at me. The Italian tilted his head, offered an inquisitive look, and smiled softly. He waved his open palms for me to continue. I took a hit of beer and eyed the package of hot dogs, surprised I was still hungry.

"Did you get to any of the islands?"

"I saw Mykonos from the ferry when it dropped off passengers, and spent time on Santorini, Rhodes, and Crete."

The Italian leaned forward in his chair and raised his beer can at the mention of Crete. He exhaled a chest-full of cigarette smoke.

"That's where I went to University to study astrology and fell in love for the first time. Did you see any of the ruins?"

"An old palace, it started with a K..."

Devis cut in. "Knossos at Heraklion?"

"I think so." I wasn't sure because of his thick accent. "It was weird there. Again, I had Deja-vu. I must have seen the place on television."

I noticed that my father and the Cambodian had tuned it to our conversation.

"Greek women are beautiful. I can understand how you fell in love there."

Michael forced a swallow of beer and interjected.

"Oh-oh, T, you just opened a can of worms."

Dad laughed; his arm stuffed into the bag of Doritos. The Italian spoke up in an effort to defend himself.

"It wasn't that I was a womanizer or anything like that."

More laughter arose from the peanut gallery.

"Her name was Aikaterina, a fellow student, and a Greek goddess. I was mesmerized by her natural beauty, but she wasn't drawn by my good looks and charm like other women."

Michael bent over and reached into the cooler, again.

He chortled. "Oh boy, here we go."

Dad smiled and nodded. Devis took that as his cue to carry on.

"Rina, that's what I called her, refused my polite and cordial advances for a month. Frustrated, I gave up the pursuit."

Dad chirped. "Better get yourself another beer. This is gonna get heavy."

I grinned and waved him off, took a slug of beer, and nodded for the handsome Italian to continue.

"That's when she turned the tables. Women…just when you think you have them figured out. After I stopped chasing her, she acted as if she was pissed off. I thought maybe she missed all the attention, and as it turned out, I was right. I played coy and Rina asked if I didn't like her any more."

The Italian continued.

"We were at the Skinakas Observatory one night…"

My father cut in.

"Okay, Devis, we all know that's the night you got laid or fell in love or whatever. Give the kid a break, why don't you share your vast knowledge of astrology with him, and brag about your degree in star gazing."

Acting in sync, we all peered into the swath of suns and planets and moons above us, the galaxy we call the Milky Way. It was as if someone took a giant paint brush loaded with glitter and swiped the dark sky.

The Italian asked, "How many constellations can you name, T?"

I rambled off a half dozen when I heard my father chuckling.

"I told you he's pretty sharp, Devis. He could name all the planets before he learned to multiply."

The Italian didn't respond. All eyes searched the stars. I didn't want to mention the earlier sighting and was about to ask Devis if he believed in such things, when he put the question to me.

"Tell me Mister T, do you believe in extra-terrestrial life or the possibility that we're not alone in the universe?"

Chapter Eight

I didn't know what to say. I looked to my father. He was staring at me. He nodded and smiled. The other two others watched for my reaction. I wasn't comfortable sharing my earlier experience. It was something personal, a father-son thing we shared. I babbled.

"There's lots of literature and television programs on the subject. I have to admit at times I want to agree with the conspiracy theorists who talk about aliens living among us, and how our government is in on it."

Thinking about my answer, I realized I never had a serious discussion about extraterrestrials with anyone.

"Some say they built the pyramids. If they're already here among us, why are we sending messages and people into space in search of life elsewhere?"

The Cambodian and my dad remained quiet. The Italian held his poker face and asked me again.

"You didn't answer my question, T, do *you* believe?"

"I think it's a matter of logistics for me. We don't have the means or the technology to travel from galaxy to galaxy, so how can anyone or anything else?"

My father interjected.

"Maybe with something like magneto drive."

Puzzled, I threw my attention his way.

"Huh?"

"You were too young to remember, but after the war I considered staying in the military to get my engineering degree. I spent a lot of time with a guy in rehab who lost a leg to an IED. This guy talked a lot about a new propulsion system he'd been working on with the military. He called it magneto drive."

My interest was piqued.

"It's a bit technical to explain but think of how opposite magnets repel when you try to put them together."

We all listened while my father continued.

"I'm not sure about the mechanics, but my buddy said they used electricity to systematically zap multiple rows of magnets stimulating and moving them away from their opposites. Try to picture a plate full of positive magnets hovering over a plate full of negative ones. The electricity creates movement in the magnets making one of the discs hover over the other."

"Like those maglev trains?" I asked.

"I guess. I'm only saying it was a theory but imagine if they could duplicate that motion in space flight without having to burn massive amounts of fuel for propulsion. The electrical power could come from batteries charged by solar energy."

Thinking about the possibility of something like that I got up and took another hot dog from the package and stood there in thought while I skewered it. The Cambodian asked if he could have one too. I handed him my prepared weenie roaster.

"I dunno, dad, if they had that technology why not..."

The Cambodian lanced the flames with his hotdog and interjected.

"They have the technology. You've heard of Roswell New Mexico and the UFO that crashed there. The government's had years to study and tear it apart, to see what makes it tick. Then there's all the experimental aircraft scores of people have reported flying around there."

My father smiled and nodded. Devis piped up, admitted he liked his American frankfurter and asked if he could have another. Dad fixed one for the Italian and one for himself. The Cambodian and I held our tube steaks over the fire. I shielded my face from the heat.

"So, you believe the whole Roswell thing Michael?"

He swallowed a mouthful of beer and nodded affirmation.

"I have no doubt. There are too many witnesses and too many unexplained sightings taking place there and all over the world. The government thinks people are stupid and will continually deny everything until everyone stops asking questions, or they lose interest."

I heard a series of high-pitched screeches and saw flashes in the sky down the beach. The neighbours got a jump on Independence Day celebrations and set off bottle rockets.

I noticed someone with flashlights around there earlier and wrote it off to the same neighbours. The Italian commented how they thought about buying some fireworks to help celebrate, but the possible hassle at the border deterred them.

Our dialogue slid sideways to movies about aliens and the different Star Trek shows and movies. We munched on hot dogs and a bag of cheese puffs my father had kept hidden from me. I listened in on the conversation, but my thoughts were all about space travel, how cool it would be, and if I would go if given the chance.

The Cambodian asked me if he could use the boy's room. I poked my last bite and led the way to the cottage. Dad called out and told me to grab their bags and show Michael to the spare bedroom.

I waved in acknowledgement and helped retrieve the bags from the car. I saw a black SUV tucked into a driveway down the street. The side windows were blacked out, but it looked like someone was sitting in the front seat.

The grimace on Michael's face said that either his bag was very heavy or his bladder was about to burst. I showed him into the cottage and pointed out the bathroom. He dropped his bag at the door. I grabbed it and the Italian's and plopped them on the two single beds in the third bedroom. I was tidying the kitchen when the man from Cambodia came out of the bathroom. He sighed.

"I think I pissed more beer than I drank. No wonder they say we only rent the stuff."

He took in the room and commented.

"Pretty rustic eh, but a great piece of property. Maybe we should talk Devis into buying the place. I'd come back here to visit again."

I smirked at his Canadian lingo. Rustic was a good description of the cottage. It was built from local knotty pine. The wood took on a golden patina as the years passed. In the bedrooms, framed paint-by-number artwork hung on the walls. The kitchen appliances were sadly outdated, and the open concept living/dining area had a nautical theme with a collection of driftwood and shells hanging in fishing net on one of the walls.

Trophy fish crowned each doorway, every one caught in the lake and mounted for bragging rights. The Lake

Trout stretched above the back door was landed by my father before I was old enough to fish. Since then, we hooked our share of Yellow Perch and Walleye, dad's favourite eating fish.

I thought about the sighting, and the conversation with my dad and his friends about strange and unexplained phenomenon. The Cambodian stood with his hands on his hips, gawking out the kitchen window at the lake.

"Hey, Michael, you said you believe in Roswell and extraterrestrials, so do you think it's all connected to your experience at Tikal?"

He smiled.

"Your father told you about that, did he?"

"I hope you don't mind me asking, we've been talking about that kind of stuff all night."

Michael pulled one of the kitchen chairs away from the table and sat down.

"What do you want to know?"

"I'm not sure. Did you figure it out—what happened to you up there?"

"Did I figure it out? Where do I start?"

He folded his arms on the table in front of him and looked past me to the bottles of booze on the countertop.

"Is that Crown Royal? It's not too often I get to indulge in Canadian whiskey. Would you mind?"

"No problem. Straight-up or on the rocks? I'm not sure what we've got for mix."

"Crown's made to be sipped straight-up. A double please."

He waited until his glass was in hand and he'd taken a swallow before telling me his story. I took a seat across the table.

"Tikal was an eye-opener for me. A window into a closed part of my brain allowed me to see, feel, and understand things like never before. Some might call it an epiphany; an insight to a world I was part of but didn't know existed. It was like I was given x-ray vision and able to see a woman's naked body beneath her clothes. Something every man thinks about at one time or another."

I offered a flat smile and nodded. I responded just like my dad. Michael spoke sincerely. I noticed for the first time the skin on his face and arms was freckled. He was of average height and stature with a square face and jaw. His eyes were the color of the Mediterranean Sea.

He took another pull of whiskey and exhaled the after burn.

"Ah, that's good stuff. I take it your father told you I had an out-of-body experience, and I saw my own aura?"

"That's how he described it but said you weren't sure at the time."

"That's an understatement. It blew me away. Intrigued and curious, I sought out a local Mayan elder and historian. In return for lunch and a few beers he told me about the ceremonies high priests performed in the temple chamber where I had my experience.

"Commoners believed their holy men had magical healing powers. Only the upper class, the kings, priests, and noblemen, knew the secrets of the pyramids and their energy healing."

Michael caught the smirk on my face. He raised his eyebrows and took a sip of whiskey.

"I know it's hard to comprehend. There are so many things humans have forgotten over the millennia. Things we don't know about ourselves or the planet we inhabit. I'm sure you learned about inertia and gravity in physics class, but I bet no one ever taught you self-healing techniques. No one explained the flow of energy through your body and all other living things, including the earth itself."

I stared at him and considered it. I thought maybe I needed a shot of whiskey but decided against it. Everything he said sounded plausible. He wasn't making it up. My brain was in overdrive. Intrigue and curiosity turned the wheels in my head.

I'm not sure why, but I just blurted it out.

"Is that what happened to you guys in Egypt. Was there something weird at the pyramid site?"

"Pyramids."

My dad bellowed as he and the Italian came in the kitchen door.

"I see you've got the whiskey out, and you're talking about pyramids?"

"Yeah, dad, I know something happened to you in Egypt and Michael's told me of a possible link between the pyramids and energy healing."

The Italian lifted the Cambodian's glass of whiskey from the table and put it to his nose.

"Is this scotch?"

Michael answered. "No, Devis, its Canadian rye whiskey."

The Italian scrunched his face and surveyed the other booze bottles on the kitchen counter.

"I try it if you pour me one."

My father fetched a glass from the cupboard, handed it to Devis and then eye-balled me.

"So, you want to know about pyramid power?"

Chapter Nine

My father poured himself a shot of whiskey and asked if I wanted one. Wanting to be a team player, I agreed to join them. He handed me a glass and held his up offering a toast to pyramid power. We clinked our glasses together and downed the shots. The Italian's face twisted, like he'd sucked on a lemon. Everyone laughed.

He gasped, "Smooth. That's the good stuff?"

He took a swig of beer and swished it around in his mouth. I asked my father again, to tell me more about the alleged mystical power of pyramids. He turned to the back door and pointed outside with his thumb as if he was hitchhiking.

"Let's talk outside, the fireworks should be starting soon and I didn't come all the way up here to God's country to sit in the cottage. There's fresh wood on the fire and it's roaring now."

Michael and I followed my father.

Devis said he needed to use the facilities first, and he wanted to change into more appropriate clothes. Whatever that meant. His expensive white cotton shirt was wrinkled. In the light I saw how good-looking he was, his dark hair curled behind his ears and tickled his collar. His eyes were a shade darker than his olive skin and he had the physique of a soccer player.

A glow came over me, one that I hadn't felt in a while. He reminded me of a boy I met in high school; my first homosexual experience. We were at a pool party and eyed each other early in the evening. Later, as the party thinned,

I *accidentally* walked in on him in the bathroom. He wasn't shocked to see me and I wasn't his first.

I didn't have a sex drive like other boys always talked about. It wasn't that I didn't find girls attractive. I related to them but didn't feel the need to pursue them. The relationships I shared with women were always as friends first, before it ever became sexual. I didn't think I was very good at love-making with women.

My sexuality was something my mother tried to help me understand. She picked up on my feminine side when I was young and showed more interest in dolls than G.I. Joes. Dad said it was just a phase I would grow out of once in school and into sports. I sucked at sports but could out-dance most of the girls.

Kevin Jordan was a proud man, and although he helped my mother with some of the household chores, changing my diapers was not one of them. He took me out of the bath tub one day and noticed my parts didn't resemble his. I wasn't old enough to understand the conversation my parents had that day. I'm sure it involved lots of questions and concerns about my future.

Outside by the fire, dad waited until he was comfortably seated in his lawn chair before he picked up the conversation.

"T, do you remember the pyramid power craze in the seventies?"

I scrunched my face in thought.

"Vaguely, I think I read about it. One of my teachers had a crystal pyramid on her desk. I thought it was a fancy paperweight."

"It probably was. Pyramids were everywhere. People sat inside large ones, held little ones over their heads to alleviate migraines, and even joined cults to worship them. There were theories about their magical healing powers. Scientists conducted experiments and reported certain foods and animals didn't rot and actually became mummified inside pyramids."

"I remember seeing something about that on the television show Myth Busters. They replicated the experiments and called it a bust, said it wasn't true."

The Cambodian waved his beer can.

"That's Yankee television for ya, don't believe everything you see on the tube."

Dad countered, "We know how much you love Americans Michael, just remember whose country you're in right now. If I remember correctly, the coach of your Toronto Dead Leafs put pyramids under the players' bench and in the locker-room hoping it would help his guys play better hockey. Too bad Philly took the series and won the Cup that year."

The Italian re-joined us at the campfire, sporting a cappuccino-coloured cotton pullover and dark khakis. He reached into the bag he carried with him and pulled out a handful of emergency road flares. The others paid him no mind, but I was more than curious. He walked the north edge of the property and spiked a line along the beach. He came back up the south side doing the same thing and glanced at his watch.

My father adjusted himself in his chair and kept talking.

"Anyway, T, mystery has always surrounded pyramids. Take the ones in Egypt for example. There are so many others around the world and new ones discovered every day. Did you know they found them in Bosnia, Burma, and all over China, some dating back five thousand years or more?"

"I know about the one in China, where Terracotta Warriors were guarding an Emperor's tomb. Is that why they buried royalty under pyramids, so special powers would help them in the afterlife?"

Devis took his seat and answered my question.

"Some experts believed they were built as monuments to monarchs or rulers, but using Egypt as an example, they found that wasn't the case. The bigger question you should be asking yourself is how and why all those pyramids were built in the first place. Where did they get the technologies and methods of construction, that can't be replicated to this day?"

Michael tossed back his last swallow of whiskey and added.

"How did ancient people, who lived thousands of miles apart, use similar technologies and building methods, when they had no way to share their knowledge or communicate with each other?"

He got up from his chair, grabbed the poker and stabbed at the logs in the fire. Pondering his question, I turned to my dad. He watched the sparks circle up and into the sky like a swarm of fireflies. His gaze drifted beyond the white-hot embers to the stars, as if searching for something. In my peripheral vision, I saw the Italian doing the same thing.

Four

"Hey dad, didn't you and mom visit the pyramids in Mexico?"

He broke from his trance and looked at me from across the campfire.

"I took her to Mexico City. It was the place to go back then, when our dollar was like gold there. We toured Mayan and Aztec ruins and the pyramids at Teotihuacán, an ancient city believed to date back to the first century B.C."

Like a kernel of popcorn in a pan of hot oil, an ember shot from the fire and bounced off the Cambodian's shin, landing near the cooler. As if it was a nasty insect, he speared it with the poker, and turned to my dad.

"I'm envious, Kevin, I toured a lot of ruin sites in Mesoamerica but never got to see the Mexican pyramids of the Sun and Moon."

Dad smiled and nodded.

"They were impressive, like many other ruin sites. They were only partially excavated and restored, but the temples were amazing. We climbed two hundred and forty-eight steps to the top of the sixty-five-meter Temple of the Sun. Your mother and I sat there in awe, appreciating each other, and the life we had. We could see for miles. It was as if we were on top of the world."

I couldn't help myself, my lips flattened to form a big grin.

"Did you have an out-of-body experience like Michael?"

The Cambodian pointed the poker at me.

"Patience young grasshopper, wait for it…"

Dad puffed his cheeks and exhaled.

"No, but I saw something really weird along the Avenue of the Dead, on our walk to the Temple of the Moon. We stopped to look at an original wall painting on the stucco façade that once covered all the buildings. It must have been spectacular in its day.

"There was a picture of a puma. Your mother and I stopped and stared at it. There was something familiar about it but I couldn't put my finger on what. She dug her nails into my forearm, obviously thinking the same thing.

"I'll never forget the bewildered expression on her face. She pointed at the artwork and said it was the same funny-looking cat I'd drawn in kindergarten. Your grandma kept it in a scrapbook and gave it to your mother when we were married.

"I felt the hair on the back of my neck stand up. I could only stare and force a nervous laugh. She huffed and said I probably copied it from a book I saw at school. I agreed but knew better. That cat was not in any book I'd ever seen."

Chapter Ten

Before I could question or comment on my father's experience in Mexico the sky exploded with bursts of colour. Fourth of July fireworks were underway. Neighbours up and down the beach set off bottle rockets and roman candles. Mortars boomed in the distance from the show at the marina, where bigger and better explosives were shot into the air. Red, white, and blue starbursts lit up the skyline.

We turned our chairs to catch the show. My father brought fireworks to the cottage when I was younger but stopped in my late teens, saying it was better to watch everyone else's displays for free. Something cold touched my elbow. It was dad with a can of beer in his hand. He wore a smile from ear to ear, we both loved fireworks.

The Italian got up and lit the road flares. The beach and lawn took on a red hue. Thinking maybe it was a European thing, I didn't bother to ask. I sat back and enjoyed the show above and on both sides of us.

The celebration carried on until the smaller shows bowed to the huge display at the marina. Thunder from the explosions felt like punches landing on my chest. The colours from exploding gunpowder intensified, the rapid succession of thumps pounded me like Rocky working a heavy bag. It was the grand finale; my favourite part. For as long as I could remember, fireworks always hatched goosebumps on my arms.

In the distance, cheering and applause replaced the sound of the mortars. Like an early morning fog, the smoke from the finale hung over the water and crept in our direction. The smell of gunpowder and cordite was thick in the air.

The four of us sat in silence as we watched the cloud dissipate. Only the sound of our crackling fire and the slapping of tiny waves on the beach remained. The water was calmer than usual.

I saw a light appear beyond the smoke. A single yellow beacon in the distance, out on the lake. I assumed it was a late-night boater heading to the marina for the holiday weekend. The light intensified as it got closer. The boat's running lamps were an odd colour. Normally markers were white, red, or green, depending on their position on the vessel.

The lake grew eerily still. The water's surface mirrored the starry sky. The strange light continued straight toward us, not the marina. I stood up to get a better look and maybe identify the craft or vessel.

The yellow light flickered and split into three, all rapidly closing in on the shoreline. Puzzled, I glanced at the others. All eyes were fixated on the trio of lights as they lined up perfectly with the red flares on our beach.

I returned my gaze to the three yellow lights. The two on the outside split in half and changed to green, making it five lights. The two new pairs flanked the yellow on either side. There was no way they were attached to any sea-going vessel I'd ever seen. As it got closer, the yellow one grew larger. The greens remained in position.

Suddenly, there was a roar overhead and the two pairs of green lights broke off in opposite directions. One went north, and the other south along the lakeshore. The noise was deafening. Two fighter jets screamed over the cottage, in pursuit of the green lights. They banked and followed the pair that headed south.

My mouth dropped open.

"Dad, do you see…"

"Yeah…keep watching, this could get interesting."

His friends all stared at the yellow light. Its position on the horizon resembled the rising sun, but much closer, and almost within our reach. The jets returned and headed north at Mach speed. I assumed it was the same pair. Those babies could travel up to fifteen hundred miles per hour.

After the sonic distraction I turned my attention back to the lake, but the yellow light had vanished. The green ones disappeared with the air force jets in hot pursuit. Those lights moved at an incredible speed.

I heard the sound of small waves landing on the beach, and an unfamiliar voice behind me.

"That was quite a show. I heard you American's go all out on Independence Day…a nice touch for our birthday."

I must've looked like a zombie. My eyes still wide from seeing strange lights and my mouth agape for loss of words. I reached for my beer, but I had knocked it over in all the excitement.

Hoping my father could explain what just happened, I turned to him. There were now four men exchanging handshakes and patting each other on the backs.

The new visitor had the Italian's skin tone, but longer black hair streaked with grey, creeping past his shoulders. He had a glow about him, a faint halo similar to what I saw earlier when the group of three first gathered. I rubbed my eyes. It was the same shade of yellow as the light I saw on the lake. I had no words. I could only stare.

Finally, my father turned to me.

"T, I'd like you to meet Carlos Rivera, better known as the Spaniard."

There he was, the missing link—the fourth musketeer. I didn't know what to say but it dawned on me the new guy also said *our* birthday. What the hell was up with that? I stepped into the group and shook the Spaniard's hand. His eyes were the colour of rock coal, dark tunnels with no light at the end. Deep facial creases aged him more than the other three men.

"It's nice to meet you, sir, I've heard a lot about you."

"All lies I'm sure. If you want to know the truth about anything, please ask me."

I took a couple of steps back and thought about the question I wanted to ask all night. I spewed the words like the foamy beer can I gave my father.

"Why do you all keep saying *our* birthday?"

The four heads turned to me in unison and they all broke out in laughter. My dad handed the Spaniard a can of beer and offered another toast.

"Cheers to *our* birthday!"

I felt left out and a little pissed off. What was the big secret? The four men lined up side by side, eight eyes reflected the fire and studied me while my dad spoke.

"I told you earlier son, these are my brothers. We all have the same birthday."

I felt like an idiot. It was a strange coincidence to say the least. But what was I missing?

I asked my father, "So you all have the same birthday and met in the same place. That's odd don't you think?"

Dad smiled and nodded.

"It gets even weirder. Not only were we born on the same day, but the same year. From the information we've been able to gather, even the same time of day."

The Spaniard probably thought I was a freak. I couldn't shake my stunned look and was again at a loss for words.

Devis asked his friend, "Where on earth have you been Carlos, we haven't heard from you since that night in Giza. We thought you'd been arrested and taken away, but the authorities wouldn't give us any information."

Michael added. "What's with your face and hair, fall asleep in the sun every day?"

Carlos shrugged.

"I disappeared for a while and some friends took me in. Sorry you guys took all the heat in Egypt."

He looked at my father.

"I tried to stop by earlier Kevin, before Michael and Devis got here. I signalled you."

My father looked puzzled.

"What signal? How did you get here?"

"I thought you and your son saw me earlier this evening. I arrived as the fireworks ended. You were busy watching the show. Some friends dropped me off."

Chapter Eleven

I heard an engine roar, saw headlights, and a dark coloured SUV racing down the road in front of the cottage. Flashlights came up the beach from the neighbour's place. Two State Troopers walked onto our property and approached us at the campfire. They searched our faces with their flashlights. It blinded me.

The female cop went to the cottage, searched its perimeter, checked the cars in the driveway, and copied licence plates. Her partner, a big guy, asked if we'd seen anything out of the ordinary during or after the fireworks. I was about to answer the question when my father squeezed the back of my arm.

Dad shook his head and replied.

"We saw a boat offshore, taking in the fireworks. It headed towards the marina. Then two fighter jets roared past overhead as part of the show for Independence Day."

The cop stabbed dad in the eyes with a beam of light, then scanned the rest of us in turn. I was ready and shielded my face.

He asked, "Anyone else see anything strange?"

The Italian and Spaniard shook their heads and the Cambodian said, "Nope."

The Trooper looked past us to his partner and pointed to the cottage.

"Who owns this place?"

My father spoke up and nodded in my direction.

"My son and I rented the place for the long weekend. We've been coming here for years."

He noticed the cop eyeballing Carlos and Devis, the two olive-skinned faces in the group.

"These other gentlemen are visiting, we all spent time together overseas."

The female Trooper joined us and nodded to her partner. He surveyed our group one last time.

"What's with the road flares?"

Michael answered. "That'd be my doing, officer, I didn't think they'd let me bring fireworks across the border from Canada."

The cops looked at each other. They were both attractive, but if I had my pick, I would choose the woman. The young man seemed full of himself.

"Okay guys, have a nice night. And thank you for your service."

They walked back to the beach, continued north.

Dad called out, "You too, officers, we appreciate you checking up on us."

I saw another police car speeding in the direction of town. A dark sedan followed at a distance.

"Lying to the cops, dad? That's not like you."

"It wasn't a lie. I basically told him what I saw, and what he wanted to hear. Do you think I should have said there were only strange lights and no boat? That we saw UFO's? And I can't help it if he thinks we were all in the military because we spent time together overseas."

Proud of himself, he smiled.

Considering the night's events and trying to explain it to the cops, I agreed it was in our best interests not to. The group remained quiet. I had the feeling they were waiting for my reaction. How was I supposed to feel after seeing two unexplained phenomena in one night?

I sat down in my chair and felt the urge to have another drink but realized I'd sobered up and didn't need any more booze. The four men talked quietly amongst themselves. They didn't use my name, but I knew the conversation was about me.

The Spanish man came to my side and put a hand on my shoulder, his thumb rested on my carotid artery.

"You seem upset, Timothy."

I didn't answer, considering he was right. Perhaps upset wasn't the right word. Confused? Frustrated? Maybe even a bit scared. Things had happened that were more than a little strange. His hand was warm on my shoulder and his thumb pulsed on my vein. No, I was wrong. It was my own heartbeat I felt.

"Please, just call me T."

Carlos stood close and he spoke softly to me.

"Your heart is racing and I can hear the blood rushing through your body. Breathe deep and relax. Open your mind to the world around you."

It was weird. Almost as if his thumb constricted the flow of blood to my brain and forced me to slow down. I felt a warm sensation and realized what he'd said.

"What do you mean you can hear my blood flowing? That's absurd."

Michael coughed, and cut in.

"Don't doubt the Spaniard, he can hear a butterfly fart from a hundred yards."

Devis and my dad laughed. I wasn't amused but felt relaxed. Carlos reached to his side and pulled his lawn chair up close to mine. He sat on an angle, facing me.

"Your eyesight has allowed you to witness extraordinary things tonight. Now you must use your other senses, smell and hearing for example. Tools you were born with but have dulled or faded away over the years. We all have the ability. Detach yourself from what you think you know and relearn how to use the special gifts born in all of us."

"What are you talking about? I'm open-minded and my senses are normal."

"Why do you struggle so hard with your sexuality? You are man and women. Are you not bi-sexual, a hermaphrodite?"

I felt blood rushing to my face and turned to glare at my father. Only a few people knew of my condition. I heard and read about the latter term but nobody had ever called me by it. Dad raised his eyebrows and shook his head. He let Carlos continue.

"Your father told me nothing. I sense your frustration and confusion, and I can smell both male and female pheromones excreted by your body. You think you're a freak of nature but in reality, you're a rarity, like a five-leafed clover."

My mother used to say I was special, but I always considered myself weird. My father never talked about it. As far as he was concerned, I was his son. I should have been angry, but I felt no animosity toward Carlos. Oddly enough, I never met anyone who could calm me like that and leave me feeling so peaceful. It was as if his soft gaze and gentle touch hypnotized me.

"I've heard about your grandmother. Are you some kind of voodoo witchdoctor like her and you just put me under your spell?"

The man from Spain offered me a flat smile. His eyes narrowed as they probed deeper into my soul.

"She was a healer and I learned a lot from her. The woman could run her hands over your body and say exactly what ailed you. We are alive with the flow of energy. Some people can feel it and others can see it. Have you heard about Michael's experience in Tikal when he saw his aura?"

"Yeah, but..."

"Were you able to see the glow around us as I arrived, when the four of us stood together?"

The Spaniard freaked me out. He was right on with what I noticed earlier and didn't comprehend at the time. His confidence came honestly. I thought about everything he said. I palmed my face with both hands and massaged my forehead and temples with my fingers like I was trying to remould my face.

"Forgive me if I seem sceptical, it's been quite a night. I had a bit to drink and it's a lot to take in. The stories, meeting all of you, and two UFO sightings. I feel like my head's going to explode. I know I'm still young and have a lot to learn but I never thought I'd have to rediscover the world in one night."

A light breeze washed over me. I heard waves slapping the beach harder than earlier in the evening. Dad poked at the fire with his stick while the Cambodian added a log to the inferno and a beer to his empty hand. The Italian gazed at the Spaniard, glad to see his long-lost brother. I replayed the night's events in my head and tried to make sense of it all.

"So, tell me dad, what's so special about the four of you, besides a birthday in common? Mathematically, it's not that big of a deal."

My father was about to answer, but Michael grabbed his arm.

"Let me say something first, Kevin. You say mathematically? Considering there are seven and a half billion people on the planet, you're right, I've done the math too. Approximately three hundred and sixty thousand people are born each day. I agree it's not a big deal. Let me go further. That makes two hundred and fifty births per minute, and again nothing special. But there only *four* people born each second."

I considered the numbers. It made sense, but I didn't see where he was going. He continued with his lesson.

"I can see you're not sold. Think about it. *Four* babies in one second, all of us male and born on the *fourth* of July, under Cancer, the *fourth* constellation. Consider the number *four*. It's the only numeral that contains the same number of letters. There are *four* cardinal points…north, south, east, west, and *four* winds.

The number *four* is the symbol of the cross, and there are *four* letters in God's name in Hebrew, JHVH. There are *four* elements and *four* true races according to the Egyptians. I could go on. In relation to us it's about four men, from four different countries and walks of life, who were drawn to the world's most famous four-sided pyramid on *our* birthday, the..."

I finished his sentence. "Fourth of July."

Chapter Twelve

Pyramids, UFO's, numbers, and the four men sitting around the campfire with me; it was a night of incredulous stories and events I had difficulty wrapping my mind around. My father and his friends tried to tell me something. I was pretty sure I knew what it was, but hesitant to make the connection. It went against everything I believed my whole life. I looked at dad. He wore a silly grin, no nod or smile.

"I know it's a lot to absorb son, but you're in the line of succession, and you need to understand what we're all about and what you're all about. Michael has three daughters and Devis had a son who died in a boating accident. Carlos has no children he knows of, so that leaves you, our only male heir. You're the end of our bloodline."

"What?" I looked at my father like he had two heads. "Bloodline? You think we're all related?"

The weirdness got even weirder. An African-American, two Europeans and a white dude wanted me to believe they were all my kin, born at the exact same time. What the hell were they smoking while I was in the cottage? I thought about it, shook my head, and scanned their faces. All attention focussed on me.

The Italian spoke up and changed the subject.

"T, do you believe money can buy anything?"

"I've heard, except for maybe love and happiness."

He forced a laugh and exhaled cigarette smoke he'd just taken in.

"Okay, I'll give you that. I knew many years ago I was put on this earth for a reason and my accumulation of wealth helped me understand. Did your father tell you about my experience in Pompeii when I worked at an archaeological site?"

"Yes, if you mean the thing with the plaster mummy. From what I understand it was Deja vu."

Devis shifted in his chair, flicked ash towards the fire.

"A feeling yes, but also a vision of something greater than myself. The same blood pumping through my veins also flowed through that little girl's body."

I thought about it for a second while he paused.

"Like re-incarnation?"

"No, not like that. It was as if someone or something wanted me to know my bloodline was the same as the people of Pompeii, and my ancestors lived and prospered there before Mount Vesuvius erupted and wiped them out. I came to believe a branch of my family tree survived and settled elsewhere."

"That's a profound idea."

The Italian nodded in agreement and sucked the butt down to its filter.

"I digress, let me get back to what money has bought me. Information. Take China for example. It is a very private country that likes to keep secrets from the rest of the world. Tourism is still limited in certain areas, but I was able to buy my way into places very few foreigners know about.

"The Chinese call theirs the Great Pyramid, and although it's the largest and oldest in the world, it was only discovered, by westerners, during the Second World War. It's where I found Dropa Stones; have you heard of them?"

I shrugged and shook my head. Devis cleared his throat and reached for the pack of smokes in his shirt pocket.

"They are stone discs discovered in mountain caves on the borderland between Tibet and China. Archaeologists unearthed seven hundred and sixteen grave sites, each one containing skeletal remains and a Dropa Stone. What's really interesting is the skeletons were only four-feet, four-inches tall, and slender with oversized heads."

"You're suggesting they were aliens?"

"You tell me. The scientist who made the discovery was afraid he'd be ridiculed if he disclosed the truth of his find. He reported the graves contained a breed of mountain gorillas. The only problem with his theory was that no gorillas ever wrote on stone discs or buried their dead in cemeteries.

The Dropa Stones are about a foot wide and a third of an inch thick with a hole in the center, similar to an old vinyl record. Someone engraved them in an unknown language using unidentified tools. They are believed to be twelve thousand years old.

Chinese scientists later reported they decoded the stones, but the results were so fantastic, Beijing refused to publish the results. Backed by his colleagues, the Archaeologist said the inscriptions described how an extraterrestrial race called the Dropa descended from the clouds in air gliders and crashed in the mountains while exploring earth."

I had to admit it was farfetched, but I was intrigued.

"So, you do mean aliens."

A quick glance around the campfire showed everyone nodding in unison. They were all believers and I was finding it difficult not to be. Devis couldn't resist the urge and he propped another fag between his lips and continued with his tale.

"I travelled to China and Tibet to satisfy my curiosity. I met a village elder in the mountains of Tibet who offered me a trade. A Dropa stone for one of my Sherpa's pack-mules, half of my supplies, a pair of Ray-bans, and a pack of Camel cigarettes.

"According to the old man, the stones were passed down through generations, along with stories of odd-looking little people who were chased from their caves by Mongols."

"He actually gave you one of the stones?"

Devis closed his eyes, smiled flatly, and nodded.

"My stone is hidden away in a safety deposit box. Do you want to see a picture of it?"

I glanced at my father. He raised his eyebrows and did his thing.

"Sure," I said. "Why not?"

The Italian pulled out his mobile telephone, turned it on and flipped through a collection of photos.

"Here it is."

He handed me the phone. I studied a photograph of a greyish-brown disc-shaped stone with a hole in the center. The inscription made no sense to me. The letters weren't from any familiar alphabet. What I did recognize were the etched figures of what appeared to be alien beings and a saucer-shaped object. They were depicted in a star-studded galaxy; not the Milky Way.

"Cool, but how do you know it's the real deal?"

Devis grinned, pinched the cigarette from his lips with his thumb and forefinger and rolled it between them.

"Money. I had it examined by professionals, cost me ten grand to learn that it's the real deal."

I handed his phone back, stood by the fire, and searched the faces of my father and his brothers from different mothers.

"Okay dad, what can I say? You guys tell a tall and convincing tale, and when I consider what else has happened tonight, I want to believe. But before I admit to anything I have to know. What the hell happened to you guys in Egypt?"

Chapter Thirteen

Michigan State Troopers Cathy Walker and Tom Howe headed for the Petoskey City Marina, as ordered. Their Captain, who they'd never seen out of the office after sun down, told them to meet him there. He was waiting with other law enforcement officials.

The drive along the lakeshore was uneventful, considering the earlier reports of strange lights in the sky. Howe was behind the wheel of the marked cruiser.

"What do you think, Cat?"

He liked to call her that, but she wasn't crazy about it. Walker stared through the windshield and answered her partner.

"Are you asking me if we've been invaded by aliens, or if it was the usual drunken tourists freaked out by the Northern Lights again?"

"You never know, I've met people who swear they've seen UFO's over the lake. But you're probably right. Maybe it was the fireworks, the starbursts and colors were impressive this year."

Walker eyed her rookie partner. Like most gun-ho newbies he would have been happier posted to a bigger and busier district, but he had to settle for directing holiday traffic in and around the state parks in Upper Michigan.

Tom normally heeded Cathy's guidance and advice. She suspected he had an ulterior motive similar to her other male co-workers—to get into her pants. Not that she would mind if he wasn't her trainee and a fellow cop. She'd already had a work relationship that ended in a painful divorce.

Like soldiers, Troopers liked to call each other by their surnames or nicknames. Walker referred to Howe as Tom or partner to make him feel like he belonged and he was an equal in their patrol unit. Almost. It's not that he wasn't a capable cop, but Howe was young and inexperienced so it was only fitting she call him rookie or newbie so he'd know his place.

Tom Howe wore the smile of a teenage boy who saw his first pair of bare boobies. Walker was probably old enough to be his mother, and a cougar to him. She was proud of her taught figure, natural blonde hair, and the high cheekbones a Hollywood actress would kill for.

"So, Cat, what did you think of that group of guys at the old white cottage down the road?"

"Not much, why do you ask?"

"I'm not sure…a gut feeling maybe. I know I'm new at this, but in all my time at the National Guard I've never seen grunts that looked like those guys."

"Old soldier's look like all other old men, grey or no hair and beer-bellies."

"Yeah, I guess so, but those two olive-skinned fellows…"

Walker cut him off as they pulled into the marina parking lot.

"Holy shit! Check it out, looks like a cop convention down there. What the hell?"

Howe pulled up amongst the other government vehicles. Their captain emerged from the group and waved them over. There were two more State Police cars, local Sheriff's vehicles, EMS, two black SUV's and a couple of volunteer firefighter pickup trucks.

The Troopers elbowed their way into the group and nodded to the Captain. He confirmed they received several calls about suspicious or unidentified lights over the lake, and along the eastern shoreline. He said some residents reported multiple sightings of UFO's.

Before the Captain could finish two government-type men in dark suits stepped in front of him. The older one advised the group there would be no mention of the words unidentified flying objects.

All reports were unconfirmed and only speculation. He said sightings of the Aurora Borealis were quite common in the area, and the holiday fireworks and accompanying light shows were the probable foundation of the reported incidents.

One of the Sheriffs didn't buy the explanation and loudly objected. The State Police Captain tried to speak up again, but more interjections from various government agencies sparked a heated argument that went nowhere.

Tongues flapped and fingers pointed. Howe gave Walker the eye. She shrugged and tilted her head toward their cruiser. They were about to climb in when the Captain and two other Troopers came over.

He was concerned about the G-men in suits and plain clothes, wondered who they really were. They flashed ID that looked like FBI. He asked his officers to take another run down the beach, keep their eyes and ears open, and talk to the residents again. The Captain waved off the group as if it were a swarm of bees and walked to his own car.

Walker snickered when her boss spun his tires and flung gravel at the other government cars. She climbed into their cruiser, beside Howe.

"Well Tom, maybe you were right about the UFO's. Those Agents sure didn't want anyone to talk about it."

"I wasn't serious when I said it earlier. I was only repeating what I'd heard from other folks. It would be cool to see something like that though, don't you think?"

Cathy Walker snorted.

"Drive rookie, you've seen too many Star Wars movies."

Chapter Fourteen

My father raised his beer can and belched a toast.

"To Egypt and the Great Pyramid."

We all laughed. Apparently, men from all over the world think burps and farts are funny. My dad was a master belcher. He could recite the whole alphabet without pause, something he was quite proud of. When my mother was around, she scolded him and told him it was rude, but she couldn't help laughing.

He dropped his chin and eye-balled me.

"Seriously, my trip to Egypt helped me understand everything we've seen and talked about tonight. What my life is all about, and what the five of us are all about. I learned there were forces of nature and universal influences that painted our lives on a huge canvass. We are tiny brushstrokes in the giant picture of life."

The sounds of crickets chirping, waves lapping, and wood crackling faded away. Only father's voice resonated in my eardrums. I was never so attuned to his words. It was as if my mind was parched and thirsty for wisdom. His eyes told the story before the words escaped his lips.

"I don't have to tell you how devastated I was when your mother died. You were old enough to feel your own pain, but not mine. She was the only woman I ever loved. Not only were we husband and wife but best friends and soul mates. When your aunt said she'd take you to give me some time to myself, I knew I had to get away.

"Looking through a box of photos one night I came across the old scrapbook that your grandma made for me. She put together one for each grandchild. They contained newspaper clippings of important events in our childhood and artwork we constructed in school. I came across my drawing of the big cat your mother and I saw in Mexico. There were hints a child drew it, but my depiction of the Puma was identical to the ancient one painted centuries earlier.

"The look on her face that day was etched in my mind. Neither one of us would admit it but we knew there was a special connection. I browsed the internet and researched the animal and the Mayans, and somehow got sidetracked on an Egyptian link. That's when it hit me. I wasn't sure why but I knew I had to go there."

A quick scan of the other faces around the fire revealed all attention was on my father. The Spaniard caught my gaze and winked. The Cambodian poked at the fire while he stared across it. I focussed on dad while he continued.

"I packed my army duffle bag and booked a flight to Cairo. I printed off maps and information from the net so I could tour the country on my own. I didn't want the company of a busload of tourists. I wanted to be alone. Like when you went to Europe, I had no set agenda, only a list of things to see and do.

"I wasn't sure about the City of Cairo. It was too big for me, with over twenty million people. The centuries-old buildings were cool to see. I wandered through a couple of museums and the old market to get a taste of the history and culture, but once I caught a glimpse of the pyramids, I knew that was where I needed to be.

"I rode the bus to the suburb city of Giza. The plateau is home to the Sphinx and the three most popular Egyptian pyramids. I had no idea at the time there were one hundred and thirty-five more of them in the country."

"A hundred and thirty-five!" I exclaimed.

Dad sat up straighter.

"Yep, and over two hundred more in the Sudan. Like we talked about earlier, they're all over the world. The three monuments were impressive even from a distance and stark reminders of an ancient world. Desert surrounding the plateau reminded me of Iraq, except there was no one shooting at me.

"The Sphinx was awesome and another mystery. Older than the pyramids and carved from solid bedrock, nobody knows why it was constructed or exactly when. The face was changed at least once in ancient times to resemble the presiding pharaoh. In our century, it was rumored a German tank blasted its nose off during the Second World War. The truth is a jealous king defaced the monument in the fourteenth century.

"I wandered the plateau in awe for hours. Coming across a group of tourists led by an English-speaking guide, I tagged along to learn more. I was astonished and amazed, probably the same way you felt the first time you saw Tiger Stadium."

The Italian waved a hand, like he was slicing the air in front of him.

"No matter how anyone describes it, T, you have to see Giza for yourself to truly appreciate its grandiosity."

My father slid to the edge of his seat and rested his elbows on his knees. In the campfire light his face appeared to be cast in bronze.

"I took in every word the guide spewed. He looked sideways at me a couple times, probably trying to remember if I was a paying member of his group. We parted company at the big pyramid, where I decided to climb to the top. It was legal back then and an arduous task, almost as challenging as army boot camp.

"The hand-cut sandstone blocks were the size of cars, stacked neatly to form a massive triangle the size of ten football fields. Stairs were carved into the bottom stones, allowing easy access to the pyramid entrance.

"I wanted to go inside but didn't have the foresight to pay for the extra ticket. I continued my ascent to the top instead. The next two thirds of my climb was the worst. There were no stairs, only a difficult climb up a huge stack of giant building blocks.

"Out of breath with scuffs on my shins and knees, the view at the top made the climb worthwhile. Nothing but clear sky and desert for miles, I thought I could see the curvature of the earth. The other two pyramids appeared much smaller from my lofty seat on top of the world.

"The huge grey stones acquired a golden hue as the earth rotated away from the sun. I could only imagine how impressive the monuments were in their infancy when the exterior was covered in white limestone. I was lost in time until shadows crept up the slope below me. It seemed wise to make my way back down before darkness made it too dangerous.

"Arriving at the bottom, I realized I barely ate that day, and a celebratory beer was in order. I wandered the streets of Giza and stumbled upon a Budweiser sign in the window of a small pub. Bellying up to the bar, I asked the blond-haired white guy on the next stool if the local beer was any good. He said the Sphinx beer was palatable and cheap, and a lot better than that America swill, Budweiser."

Michael chuckled and was about to defend himself but my father raised a finger to him and carried on.

"The bar had no identity. Advertised out front as a pub, the inside was like the man-cave we created at my first army base in Iraq. Stacks of empty beer cases panelled the back wall. Tables and chairs didn't match and looked like lost treasures purchased at garage sales.

"The bar consisted of one long slab of rock and must have weighed a ton. It was probably stolen from an old ruin site. A door-less wooden armoire stood behind it and held an impressive collection of bottled liquor.

"Acting on my stool-mates recommendation, I asked the bartender for a Sphinx. Mine was the darkest shade of skin in the bar and I wondered if whitey was prejudice because of his country and beer comment. The cold brew passed my lips and slid down my throat as fast as I could deliver it. A nice treat in a Muslim country where alcohol is mostly forbidden. I finished in a few big gulps. The server raised an eyebrow and I nodded for another.

"I scanned the room and saw paper money from every country in the world stapled to the walls and furniture. The blonde guy downed a shot of clear liquid. I caught a whiff of black liquorice and asked him what he was drinking. He smiled and signalled the bartender for two more hits. I said he didn't have to do that, but he replied they were birthday shots.

Four

"Perplexed, I asked him how he knew it was my birthday. Baffled by my question, he offered his hand and said he was celebrating his birthday. He introduced himself as Michael Carter, a Canadian expat currently residing in Cambodia."

As my dad took a breath, I turned to look at the dual citizen. He raised his eyebrows but remained quiet, enjoying my father's version of events. Dad continued after the brief pause.

"We shook hands and our shots were delivered. Michael asked how I liked the beer. I said I was thirsty and it went down easy but tasted bad. He snorted and said it was recycled camel piss and Budweiser was way better. I knew right then and there he was a wise-ass. We shared a laugh and toasted our birthday.

"Michael shared his expertise in fine brews and said none of the local beers were any good. He ribbed me about my American accent. I was about to throw an insult his way when I noticed the bartender staring at us. I responded with a glare. He broke eye contact and turned his attention on two other men seated at a table behind us.

"Returning to pick up our empty glasses he nodded toward the other men and asked in broken English if we were all having a birthday party. When Michael asked what he was talking about, the bartender pointed to the other two guys and said they were also celebrating a birthday."

Chapter Fifteen

My father couldn't help himself; his relaxed pose revealed his fondness for the memories of Egypt. In a glance I saw the other men had the same demeanor. They were at peace with the world and their place in it.

Something different about the Spaniard still nagged at me, but I couldn't put my finger on it. Like he was holding something back. Something secret. Who was I to wonder, I barely knew the man.

The Cambodian couldn't contain himself and he took over the narration.

"Imagine our surprise when we found two more men in the same bar with the same birthday. We invited ourselves to their table to wish them happy birthday. When I explained that we all shared the same date of birth they looked at us like we were from another planet."

I sat back in my chair and shook my head, amazed at the freakish coincidence. The Italian grew animated and waved his cigarette like a conductor's baton to add his recollection of the event.

"At first I thought it was a joke. It was unbelievable but for some unknown reason, acceptable. Carlos and I met years earlier while scuba diving at the underwater pyramid near Portugal. We..."

I snapped back.

"Underwater pyramid in Portugal?"

Devis discarded what was left of the cancer stick and nodded.

"It may be the biggest and oldest one discovered yet, some believe it's the lost City of Atlantis. Anyway, Carlos and I met on a dive there. We didn't know we shared the same birthday until we were accidentally reunited on the street outside the same bar where we met your father and Michael. How do you like those odds?"

The number four danced around in my brain. Four men, four countries, and four births on the same day. I grew light-headed thinking about it.

My dad cut in.

"From the moment we introduced ourselves I felt connected to these guys. After we got past the birthday thing, we each talked about our reasons for being in Egypt. Our past experiences brought us there. I didn't feel worthy, these men had travelled and seen so much more than me."

The Cambodian stood and headed to the cooler for another beer. He took the opportunity to continue with his version of the chance meeting.

"It was a no-brainer once we shared our strange stories and tales. It was obvious to me a greater force brought us all together in the same place, on the same day—our birthday. We all saw similar parts of Egypt since being in the country, and agreed there was something inside the great pyramid of Khufu that we were all destined to see. It was a calling none of us could describe or ignore."

My father stifled a burp so he could talk. Nobody laughed.

"That's when Devis said he knew a guy who could get us inside the great pyramid. He once worked with a member of the archeological team who discovered a new chamber. It was a state secret and no one was saying what, if anything, was inside the space.

"The Italian and Spaniard already toured inside the monument and knew the layout. We were all aware there were passageways and rooms, and even tunnels in and under the pyramid, but the newly-discovered cavity was a mystery we had to explore."

The campfire smoke drifted my way again. I rubbed my eyes to clear my vision and considered the current events. It was fun. Not only had I witnessed UFO's, but I met three men who were kind of like my uncles and shared the same birthday as my father. Their story was starting to sound like an Indiana Jones movie.

The Italian took the reins and carried on with his recollection of that night.

"It's like I said earlier about money, the right amount in the right hands can unlock doors and get you into places where no one else is allowed. The new chamber was a state secret, something authorities wanted to keep quiet until they had a chance to explore it further. For reasons unknown the Egyptian government has released less and less information as they discover more and more about the ancient monuments.

"Archaeologists and pyramid experts speculated for years about more secret rooms and chambers that were yet to be discovered. In some respects, I don't think we can blame officials for secrecy when you consider past grave and tomb robberies.

"Over the centuries valuable information and artefacts were destroyed, stolen, and lost forever. On the other hand, I feel we have a right to know the truth, especially after the all the false and incorrect information historians have led us to believe."

"Okay, let me get this straight." I said. "By chance you all met in a bar in Egypt, discovered you had the same birthday, pounded shots over strange stories, and decided to sneak into one of the world's greatest historical sites?"

The Spaniard got up from his chair, stretched his back and turned his head from side to side to relieve the kinks in his neck. He stared at the black curtain drawn across the lake.

The man was noticeably different from my father and the others. He was more distant, as if his mind was focussed on something else. His eyes found mine and he answered my question.

"We all felt the same. We were drawn together and it was meant to be. It was the same with our interests in the pyramid. We were summoned by someone or something greater than ourselves. It was our destiny and there was no doubt in any of our minds we had to get inside that monument, whatever the cost."

Carlos went on, telling me about how the archeological team used new technology and special x-rays to discover a new empty chamber above the Grand Gallery.

"That's what the two men in charge led the rest of their team to believe. Devis' guy overheard them talking about an anomaly inside the void, and how the machine's penetrating rays were reflected back by something inside. The two scientists tried to keep their test results from the team, but the guy saw a photo image of a triangular-shaped object inside the vault.

They disagreed on what the anomaly or object might be, because their instruments showed metallic readings. In considering its size, one of the experts thought it might be the long-missing capstone from the top of the pyramid, rumored to be cast of solid gold.

"That theory was credible considering the newly-found void mimicked the Grand Gallery below it and ran parallel in an upward direction. The hidden passageway could have been used as a ramp to carry the finishing stones to the top of the pyramid.

"Devis had known his source for years and trusted him implicitly. The man was reluctant to share the information but felt obliged because our Italian friend had introduced him to the beautiful woman who later became his wife. He said the guards were lazy and the one at the pyramid entrance could easily be bribed to turn his back. He even supplied a map of the passageways and the location of the newly-discovered chamber."

My father got up and fetched the poker. He said they made a joint decision to stop drinking that night, knowing they'd need their wits about them to pull off such a caper. The bartender looked suspiciously at them when they moved to a private corner table to carry on their conversation and look over the Italian's map.

Dad said he felt like he was back in the army with the Italian as his sergeant, briefing the platoon on their plan of attack. How to out-flank the guards and get past the security cameras to penetrate enemy territory. Devis was the man with the plan but the rest of the group was ready and willing to do whatever was required to get inside that pyramid.

"I know it sounds selfish, that I didn't consider the consequences. I had a son at home who needed me, but it was something I had to do for myself. That's why I'm telling you all this. Why you need to know about the four of us, and more importantly what it will mean to you."

What it would mean to me?

I wasn't exactly sure what it was all about but I was content to listen. The story was just getting good; Indy was about to discover the hidden treasure. My father was more animated than I'd ever seen him. The closest he ever got was at Tiger games when he'd get excited and jump out of his seat to yell and scream at the umpire when he didn't agree with a call. He was different now, his wide eyes and taut face expressed joy and he looked twenty years younger.

"I wish you could have seen us. Four grown men, complete strangers, huddled around a map that would take us to a place hidden and undiscovered for thousands of years. Trouble was we had no idea what was in that room or exactly why we all felt it was our mission to look inside. A plan was hatched. We should have had more questions and concerns but we didn't. We knew our destiny awaited us."

Chapter Sixteen

Troopers Walker and Howe drove south along the lake road, toward Petoskey State Park. Classic rock from a station in Traverse City played on their car radio. Walker tapped on the armrest and hummed to the music until the announcer broke in with a news flash. He said several callers reported strange lights and air force jets in the sky over Lake Michigan.

The DJ added how calls to other stations had been received from people as far away as Gary, Indiana. Howe remained quiet while he absorbed the news report. He glanced at his partner. The music returned and Walker resumed tapping and humming. She recognized the intro for the next song and pressed her lips tight to conceal her smile. David Bowie's Space Oddity played on the stereo.

Howe continually shifted his eyes between the road in front of him and the sky above, searching. Walker couldn't resist and sang to him, adding her own lyrics.

"Ground control to Trooper Tom…take your pills and put your helmet on…there are calls for strange lights in the air…it's time to leave the cruiser if you dare…"

She snorted and laughed out loud at herself. Howe did his best to give her a dirty look but his reddened face cracked a smile. He was like a big kid and at times Walker felt like she was his mother.

"C'mon Cat, you heard the radio. Why do you think the G-men and Air Force jets are buzzing around here? Do you think everyone's wrong or mistaken about what they saw?"

"A wise man once told me you can't believe everything you hear, and only half of what you see."

Howe scoffed.

"You mean you wouldn't believe your own eyes if we saw a UFO tonight?"

Walker bent forward and turned the music down.

"I'm just saying there's too much hype. The media hears about it and blows it out of proportion, and everyone believes it must be true because they saw it on television or heard it on the radio.

"People are gullible and they believe whatever they're told. You've seen how they buy the bullshit we feed them, like telling them how safe they are, regardless of the known criminals or perverts who live in their neighbourhood."

"I don't know, Cat, not all people are as naïve as you think."

The forested stretch along the highway cooled the night air. Walker caught the scent of pine as she closed her window.

"Okay, Tom, you're a smart guy. Tell me the facts. What proof is there of extraterrestrials?"

He thought about everything he'd read.

"There's been plenty of proof all over the world, but it always gets covered up by the government, like those guys in the suits. Did you see the movie, Men in Black?"

Walker laughed out loud.

"Did you forget you work for the government, partner? And yeah, I saw the movie with my nephew. I thought it was lame. You think we have a secret immigration office where they keep tabs on alien traffic to and from earth?"

Howe shook his head, flexed his forearm, like he was going to give her a backhander.

"Alright, alright...maybe that movie is a bad example...except for those guys in the suits. But you're right, we do work for the government, and I know for a fact that you don't always believe what you're told. Don't believe everything you hear—sound familiar?"

"Okay, partner, I'll put this to rest and admit there are things on this planet and elsewhere in the universe I don't understand. It doesn't mean I believe in aliens. UFO's are just unidentified objects in the sky."

She remembered something and giggled to herself.

"What?"

"Okay, there was one time. My sister and I were sitting in the park at the end of our street smoking a joint."

She put a hand up to stop Howe from interjecting.

"My sister talked me into trying it. Anyway, we were listening to music when what we thought was a spaceship flew over the treetops. Freaked out but curious, we jumped on our bikes and chased it through the neighborhood."

Howe raised his brow.

"The thing moved quietly and slow enough for us to keep up. We followed it for a couple of blocks until it stopped over a streetlight. The sky was dark above the lamp but I could make out the size and shape of what looked like a smaller version of the Goodyear Blimp.

"It just hovered there. We hid in the bushes waiting to see if it would land and giggled about the prospect of meeting little green men. Eventually we got brave enough to toss a few stones at it. That's when they threw a rope down from the ship. We just about peed ourselves. A car whizzed by and its headlights revealed the rope was snagged on the light post.

"My buzz had worn off by that point so I talked my sister into boosting me up the pole so I could reach the rope. I pulled and my sister screamed when the ship slowly floated down to us. Turns out it was a large advertising balloon and we had a close encounter of the zeppelin kind."

Walker's partner chuckled but his face showed disappointment at the ending of the story. She shook her head.

"So, there you go—you can't even believe what you think you see. We did get our pictures in the paper and a reward from the advertising company for capturing the blimp. Apparently, it traveled two counties after breaking away in heavy wind."

Howe tried to remember if he had a comparable story but his thoughts were interrupted by the dispatcher. She requested they respond to an address on cottage row in the area they checked earlier, for a report of strange yellow lights over the lake.

Walker palmed the microphone and responded, 10-4. She dared not look at Howe, and knew he'd be wearing a celebratory grin. She resumed tapping the armrest.

He asked, "What's with the tapping you always do? It's not in sync with the music."

"Morse Code. Something my father learned in the navy and passed on to me. It's a habit, I pick words out of a song and repeat them in code."

She tapped on the armrest. - --- --

"What does that mean?"

"It's the letters of your name: T O M."

The Troopers weren't far off and arrived at the address within minutes. A blue-haired old woman wearing a red, white and blue house coat flagged them down when they rolled up to her driveway. Howe was out of the car and standing in front of the woman before Walker finished advising dispatch of their arrival.

The old woman was animated, she waved her arms as if trying to swat mosquitoes buzzing around her head. After she got out of the car, Walker quick-marched to catch up to her partner and the complainant, who were headed down her driveway toward the lake.

When she caught up the old woman was out of breath, telling Howe he just missed the yellow lights flying south over her beach.

"Just like the ones on the radio." She said. "I missed them earlier when I was taking my bath, but then I came outside to see what was going on."

The Troopers looked up and down the beach seeing nothing but nodding in agreement to appease the woman. It was another lame call, and waste of their time.

The woman gasped. "Look here they come again!"

She was right. It was a group of three yellow lights off-shore, hovering a few hundred feet over the beach and coming their way. Howe stared, his mouth agape. Walker checked his reaction and smiled. She turned to the robed woman as the lights neared them.

"Look really close when they fly overhead ma'am. Can you see the little flames underneath the yellow lampshades? They're paper kites, called Chinese lanterns.

People light them on the beach and set them adrift in the sky."

The woman held her expression of amazement. Howe stood with his hands on his hips and frowned like a kid who just had his favourite toy taken away. Walker fought the urge to laugh and tilted her head to signal her partner she was heading back to their car.

When Howe climbed into the cruiser, he avoided eye contact. He backed down the driveway while Walker cleared them from the call. The dispatcher acknowledged and sent them to another address further down the road where someone reported emergency flares on the beach.

"Don't people know its Independence Day?"

When she acknowledged the call, the dispatcher added that the complainant saw the same thing earlier in the evening just before the strange lights appeared in the sky.

Chapter Seventeen

The Cambodian didn't say much, his head bobbed as he listened to the conversation. He had a couple more beers and shots than the rest of us and the booze appeared to be taking its toll. Dad said the Italian led the stealth mission—the covert penetration of the great pyramid of Khufu. Devis stood, smoked, and added body language for effect.

Their source said they should take in the nighttime light show and sneak off to the restrooms one or two at a time during the performance. A short distance from the lavatories was a covered dig site where they could hide until everyone but the guards left for the night.

He added security was underpaid and usually slept through their night shifts. There was no guarantee they wouldn't stumble across one who took his job seriously and patrolled the road around the pyramids.

It was the guard stationed at the opening on the north face of the pyramid who'd been bribed and told to have a good nap after the show. The door was the only entrance to get inside and it would be nearly impossible to get by an alert guard.

Devis learned earlier in the day that security usually sat in a chair just below the doorway with their back to the wall. Even if the guard reneged on his deal, the foursome could possibly sneak in from above and behind him.

The guards worked twelve-hour shifts, with the night guys on from eight at night until eight in the morning. It was dark by nine but the light show wasn't over until after ten. It was another half hour before everyone was out and the guards settled into their assigned areas. It would have been safer to wait until security bedded down for the night, but the four men all felt they had to be in place, wherever that was, before midnight and the end of their birthday.

By 11:00 pm they could wait no longer. The fearless foursome had darkness and distance and a climb up and into the pyramid ahead of them. Swallowed by the silence of the desert around them, they made their way to the western base of Khufu. The few stars visible in the night sky were obscured by clouds, and there was no moon. Conditions were perfect.

With no shadows to separate them, the huge grey stones in the wall appeared welded together. Devis checked his watch when they reached the base. In answer to his nod the four men ambled up the west wall, their plan being to gain some height and move around to the north face where they'd be above and behind the sentry at the entrance. From that position they'd be able to sneak in behind him.

Devis acted out the climb up and over the huge blocks of stone.

My dad interjected and said some were almost the size of the cottage and they wondered how the ancient Egyptians moved and stacked them so many years ago. He realized how out of shape he was but took solace in the fact he wasn't the only one having trouble negotiating the giant stones in the dark.

It took them a bit longer than anticipated but they were happy to see the guard in his chair, positioned far below them at the bottom of the north wall. Once inside the door, they paused to catch their breath, and exchange pats on the back.

A dark passageway led them into the pyramid, and their destiny. Staying quiet and using only hand signals, the Italian inched forward, feeling and using one wall as a guide until they were far enough inside to activate their lights. Someone made ghost sounds and the others giggled like school children in sex-education class. The Italian shushed them.

Devis switched on his flashlight, and the others followed suit. They stood in the Grand Gallery, a passageway connecting the King and Queen's chambers. The Spaniard explained how experts believed the Egyptians used it as an interior ramp during construction of the huge monument. The smooth stone walls tapered in towards a high ceiling their beams of lights could barely reach.

My father and Michael walked downward into the Grand Gallery, but Devis called for them to stop. He waved them in the other direction, towards the King's chamber. Carlos disappeared around a corner. When the others caught up, the Spaniard was standing in front of a makeshift gate. According to the Italian's source, that was where the x-ray technicians conducted their tests.

It wasn't a gate or doorway to anything in particular, only a slight recess in the wall where a section of blocks was out of alignment. The scientists or government officials fastened a full sheet of plywood to the stone. Official seals covered the edges on both sides. The authorities would have been wiser not to mark the area at all. The seals only aroused more curiosity.

The wood was attached to the wall with heavy lag bolts. Without proper power tools, the fantastic four had to resort to using flathead screwdrivers and small pry-bars they concealed in their backpacks.

It was a slow process, but bit by bit they pried the wood away from the wall. Eventually the bolts loosened and wobbled in their pre-drilled holes. It took all eight hands to pull the board free.

First surprise, then frustration, as more curiosity set in. There were scratches and drill marks in the stone where the scientific instruments were attached and used to probe the wall. There was no door or entranceway to anywhere. Devis tilted his head back and lit up the ceiling. There was nothing there but more solid stone.

If his source was correct the newly discovered void should be directly above them. It made sense that any access would be through a wall or another passageway. The scientists must have found a way in, why else would they seal off the wall? The Italian told the others to examine the wall closely and feel every inch of it with their fingertips. There had to be a secret entrance.

My father noticed the Cambodian wasn't helping. He stood behind the others staring at the wall. He told them to step back. Devis rubbed his fingers raw, working at the seams. He gave Michael a dirty look and got a shit-eating grin in return. He pointed to a joint in the stone.

He traced the outline of a slightly darker coloured stone, first running his finger down the left side, then across to the right. Then down the right side past the intersection of the next stone.

"Don't you see it?" He asked. "This one stone is narrower and its lines form the number four. It's our door. It has to be."

He moved closer and ran his hand along the bottom edge.

"See how it sticks out a bit here? There are grooves where it protrudes from the stone below, where it was dragged, or moved over the top."

The Cambodia glanced back at the others who stood frozen, staring at him as if he were naked.

"What are you guys waiting for? Get over here and help me push."

The four put their shoulders into the wall, and the dark stone slid back like it was on rollers. They pushed it back about two feet and felt a rush of air. Looking inside, the light from their helmets was swallowed by the black void above them.

The bottom stone on the wall and the one above it created a stairway into the abyss. An eerie silence hung over them. Without hesitation, they squeezed through the opening, and forged ahead into the ancient passage in search of the answer to all their questions.

More stairs led the men up and further into the black hole. The Italian went first. He poked his head through a doorway but his helmet barely lit up the void. The others followed him into a narrow hallway similar to, but smaller than the Grand Gallery.

Curious, they swivelled their heads in all directions, the searchlights probing the walls and ceiling. There was nothing to see except for an indiscernible object further along, near the end of the passage. They continued up the slope in that direction. As they neared the obstacle it started to take shape. It almost filled the passageway, stretching from wall to wall and floor to ceiling.

Devis stopped a few feet away and the others fanned out around him. It appeared to be a huge stone, carved into the shape of a triangle. It was a pyramid. Could it be the missing capstone from the top? Legend said it was made of solid gold. They moved in closer.

The air was heavy and still, and so quiet my father said he could hear his own heart beating. Carlos pointed out faint symbols carved into the stone, covered in thick dust. Devis and Michael used their hands to brush away thousands of years of the fine grey powder. Dad and Carlos followed suit.

The Cambodian fingered the symbols as they were revealed. A sudden jolt caused him to jump back. It felt like an electrical shock. The hair on his arms was standing on end. He asked the others if they felt anything. They were busy removing the dust, but one by one they stepped back. Wide-eyed, they nodded in unison. They'd felt it too.

Keeping their distance, they examined the symbols and hieroglyphs carved into the object. Some of the markings protruded from the stone and weren't consistent with any Egyptian script. The Cambodian called the others to his side and pointed out what appeared to be saucer-shaped objects and short people with large heads, similar to the symbols on the Dropa Stones.

The triangle-shaped object didn't appear to be made of the same material as anything else in the great pyramid. It was smoother, a silvery color, and had a metallic feel to it.

There were four identical sides with a flat bottom resting on the stone floor.

Carlos found an impression of a human right hand and he fit his own into it. When he felt his fingertips tingle, he told his brothers to search the other sides. One by one they all found similar impressions on each side. They shouted excitedly but couldn't see each other because of the size of the object.

My father found his hand was too big for the impression, so he went to Michael's side and it was a perfect fit. The Cambodian knew what to do, he had the others rotate positions until they all found the matching impression to their right hand. Everyone felt the tingling, a flow of energy. Things got weird and crazy.

Chapter Eighteen

The steady vibration almost numbed their fingertips and hands as the energy travelled up their arms and into their bodies. The sensation was warm and peaceful. The whole triangle started to vibrate, and the remaining dust fell from its sides. A low hum resonated from inside, tickling their eardrums.

The foreign object began to glow, a dull white colour at first. The Spaniard shouted to the others to keep their hands in place, as if any of them would move at that point. They all knew and felt it deep in their souls. They were meant to be there. With all the sediment gone, the pyramid's shiny silver shell was revealed.

The Italian reached up with his left hand and fingered the row of strange symbols protruding from the triangle's skin, a series of ones and zeros, like a binary code. He asked the others about their sides and they reported the same thing. Four rows of code wrapped around the object.

Devis told each of them to read out the symbols on their side. Upon completion of the last sequence, the humming stopped and the sides of the triangle became clear as glass. They could see each other, as if they were staring through an empty aquarium. The four men showed the same expression, not fear or terror but exhilaration and excitement. Emotions ran through them like electricity.

The group was connected to something larger than themselves. They shared a sense of knowing, acceptance, and peace. As if their souls had melded into one. It was nirvana and unconditional love. Could it have been heaven?

In that moment, the pyramid levitated and a speck of light appeared inside. It grew and split into four golden spheres, each choosing a man. They became one with the lights. The triangle's clear sides changed again and became reflective or mirror-like. Carlos used his other hand to touch the material, it stretched like plastic food wrap. He pushed harder and the material surrounded him like a rubber glove.

Each man witnessed something different. At first it was their own reflection. Then a collection of images throughout their lives played in reverse. The picture show traced back to the day of their birth, and then beyond to the lives of their fathers and forefathers. They saw themselves as politicians and policemen and soldiers and tribal leaders. Were they travelling back in time? Some places they recognized, others they didn't.

At the end there were four men who appeared to be siblings, offspring of a man and woman. Their features passed down over generations and thousands of years. The couple was naked, like Adam and Eve.

There was something odd about the woman's genitals, my father recognized it right off. She was a hermaphrodite—alien like his son. Dad reached out to caress the face of his mother, their mother.

Someone shouted from the end of the corridor where they'd entered the hidden chamber. Distracted, his hand slipped from the imprint. Just before the mirror returned to its original metallic colour, he thought he saw Carlos inside. The pyramid stopped vibrating and settled back onto the stone floor.

More angry shouts and beams of light came their way. Figures took shape as they got closer. They were uniformed guards. The gig was up. They told the men to step away from the pyramid.

Security lit them up with their flashlights and ordered the three of them to exit the way they had come. Three of the brothers looked at each other. Yes, the guard said three. They mustn't have seen Carlos. He was on the far side of the triangle, out of sight.

The nosy trespassers were escorted back to the secret doorway and set of stairs where they entered the chamber. No one mentioned Carlos.

Later, Michael said he glanced back at the object before leaving the room and thought he saw a faint yellow light glowing inside of it. If the Spaniard was hiding behind the pyramid, he couldn't see him.

Chapter Nineteen

Gladys Brindley was startled by the knock, she tip-toed to the front door and peeked out the tiny peep-hole. She didn't recognize the two clean-cut and casually-dressed men standing on her porch.

They couldn't be cops, the state police had already been there and made her feel like an idiot for reporting some kind of Chinese lights in the sky. She thought about calling them back to report the two intruders.

A second and closer look revealed one of the men was holding a gold badge up near the peep-hole. Anyone could get a fake these days, she thought. Gladys shouted through the door.

"Get off my porch or I'll call the police."

One of the men answered.

"We are the police, ma'am, we'd like to speak to you about your earlier report of strange lights in the sky."

She thought about what the man said. How did he know that? If they were police, they didn't look like any she'd ever seen before.

"You don't look like cops, where's your uniforms?"

The same man held up an ID card with his badge.

"We're from the Federal Investigation Bureau, ma'am, and we don't wear uniforms."

Gladys became more curious than afraid. Maybe there was more to those lights she saw. Brindley started to second-guess what she actually saw and what she was told she saw. The security chain was latched, she opened the door a couple inches. The other man held up his badge and ID.

"What do you want? I already talked to the cops about the lights over the lake. They were Chinese kites or something like that. They looked more like UFO's to me. Ain't the first time I've seen strange things over the lake, who knows what's out there. I'm an old woman, all by myself, and I've heard talk about alien abductions."

The man closest to the door put a hand up, stopping her from going on.

"Can we please come in and talk to you? There is an explanation for what you saw. We're government agents, we mean you no harm."

They said they were from the government and looked dead serious. Gladys thought their tidy appearance and handsome looks made them trustworthy. Especially the dark-haired one with the moustache. She opened the door and allowed them in.

Brindley offered a smile to the cute one. A low growl froze them in their tracks. An aged and overweight Golden Lab stared from its prone position on the couch.

"Oh, don't worry about Bear, he's deaf, half blind, and so fat and old he can barely get off the couch. Dogs, they age so quickly; seven years to every one of ours you know. He's not as spry as he used to be. I might be old too, but I take care of myself."

Gladys batted her eyes at dark and handsome, fluffed her hair up on one side. Being experienced at reading people, the moustache kept the conversation going. His partner asked if he could use the bathroom, his excuse to snoop around the house.

"Mrs. Brindley, would you be kind enough to tell me exactly what you saw over the lake earlier this evening."

"Please, call me Gladys. I haven't been a Mrs. since my husband passed away. God bless his wretched soul. Can I get you something cold to drink—iced tea or lemonade perhaps?"

"Thanks, but no Gladys, we're very busy tonight and can't stay long. We just need to know…"

"I don't know what else I can tell you. I thought I saw lights but those other cops said it was paper lanterns folks fly around for the holiday. At least that's what they said when they were here. The lights I saw earlier were different. They moved really fast and stayed in a row, like how a flock of geese fly together."

"That's why we wanted to talk to you Gladys, to let you know you're safe and what's really going on out there. It was an air force drone you saw."

"A drone? You mean like those things that drop bombs on the Muslims?"

The agent's partner returned to the living room, nodded too signal he was satisfied with his search of the house. Dark and handsome blinked to acknowledge him.

"Not quite like those drones Gladys, the one you saw tonight is for surveillance. The military uses them to take pictures and thought they'd fly one through the fireworks to simulate battle conditions. They have running lights like airplanes so they are visible from the ground and to other aircraft."

Brindley lifted her brow in thought, nodded along in agreement.

"Well that makes a hell of a lot more sense than paper kites on fire…sorry, pardon my French. Are you sure I can't get you gentlemen something cold to drink?"

"No, but thanks again. We just wanted to make sure you were safe and let you know you have nothing to worry about. Your government has everything under control. Think of it as your tax dollars at work."

His partner was already at the door, mustache turned to join him.

"Well, if you say so, I appreciate you checking up on me. Come by again when you can stay longer, I don't get many visitors these days."

"No problem ma'am, we're here to serve. You have a good night."

The agents left the house and returned to their car in the driveway. The partner chuckled and turned to dark and handsome.

"Sure you don't want to stay a while partner, isn't mature and lonely your type?"

Agent moustache checked his reflection in the mirror.

"Hey, don't knock it till you've tried it."

They both laughed and headed to their next address to quash any other stories that didn't synch with the company line.

Chapter Twenty

I hadn't noticed when, but at some point during their story I'd stood up with my arms folded across my chest. Nervous tension caused a knot in my stomach. It was as if I was in the pyramid with them. I wiped a bead of sweat from the side of my neck and felt my elevated heartbeat in my fingertips.

The campfire had been neglected as the tall tale unfolded. It wasn't the fire's heat causing me to perspire. I was tense, excited, and in awe of what I just heard. I took a couple of deep breaths to relax and regain my composure.

Carlos got up and grabbed a few pieces of wood and put them into the fire pit. He regarded the rising embers as if they were tiny spacecraft, heading to a far-off galaxy.

Devis studied his friend, as though he'd just met him for the first time. I noticed my dad and Michael gawked at the Spaniard in the same way. The four men were connected on a level I could never comprehend. The Italian got up from his chair and grabbed the bag of road flares.

We watched him lay them out on the same path he had earlier. The campfire lit the other men's faces. They were all creased with the same smile. My dad nodded. I was so curious.

"What's with the flares? The fireworks are over."

My father and Michael answered simultaneously.

"Ask Carlos."

I sat up straighter, scanned the group again, and stopped at Devis. With everything that went on, and whatever wasn't being said, I had a strange feeling something else was about to happen. When I turned and looked at the Spaniard, he was rigid in his chair. He stared into the dark and empty space above the lake, as if he could see something on the opposite shore.

Another light appeared on the horizon. A lone star sitting on the surface of the water. A white sun rising in the pitch-black sky. We all stared, our gaze locked and frozen like a deer in headlights. The star moved toward us, slowly at first, and then like a comet it came straight at us. My muscles tensed. A good thing because I almost peed my pants.

The light skimmed the water's surface stopping just short of the beach, where it hesitated for a split second and then shot straight up into the air. Our heads snapped back in unison trying to follow it.

The ground shook. At the same moment two fighter jets screamed overhead. The noise hit us about the same time as the jet wash and a spray of water from the lake. It practically blew us out of our lawn chairs.

As the sound subsided, another light appeared on the horizon. It was yellow and it followed the same path as its predecessor, coming directly at us. That's when I figured out the red flares mimicked a runway.

Waves in the black lake water stopped, its surface resembling a freshly-waxed floor. The mirror effect gave the impression of two yellow lights, one on top of the other.

No one spoke. I heard nothing at all, no crackling of burning wood or chirping of crickets. The object stopped, maybe a hundred yards off shore. It was like a brilliant sunset in an ink-black sky. The sphere settled on the water's surface and sunk below it. The reflection disappeared and the water around the object became illuminated.

It was awesome, like I was looking into a giant aquarium without the fish. The lake water was translucent. My jawed dropped when I saw the object take on the shape of a triangle. A golden pyramid. I forced myself from my trance and glanced at my father. His eyes were locked on the object, but his smile and nod told me what to do.

I kicked off my shoes, tore off my shirt, and charged toward the beach. It was hard to describe, but I felt I was on a mission to discover my own destiny. Everything I heard that night prepared me for what was out there in the lake. My stomach did back flips. I had goosebumps and tingled all over.

I swam towards the light. A low and resonating hum vibrated my eardrums. It came from the object ahead of me. I kept my head above water. I didn't want to miss a thing. As I got closer, the water around me bubbled and made me more buoyant.

I swam up to and over top of the golden pyramid. I could see it clearly, submerged and hovering over the bottom of the lake. The bubbles around me grew larger and larger and suddenly I was inside one, like a Christmas ornament.

My glass submarine descended until it rested alongside the glowing object. Concerned about air I reflexively panicked for a second, but then realized I was able to breath.

As if in suspended animation, I floated alongside the pyramid. It was about the size of a small car. I saw my reflection in its metallic-looking shell. The shiny color reminded me of something cast in gold. The bubble moved in synch with my thoughts as I circled the strange object. Then I saw it.

It was just like in the story I'd heard earlier. There was an indentation on one side of the pyramid in the shape of a hand. I instinctively knew what I had to do. My reach passed through my capsule as if it wasn't really there. My fingers remained dry as they wiggled through the water and reached for the imprint.

I pressed my hand in place. The pyramid was warm to my touch and I felt it vibrating. The rhythm changed and slowed until it mimicked my heartbeat. It was freaky but fucking amazing.

Once the object and I were in sync, the reflective sides became clear. It was an empty glass pyramid. A million questions ran through my mind. I tried to remember everything I'd heard from the foursome earlier.

In the time it took me to blink, I realized I was inside the glass triangle looking out. I breathed normally but wasn't quite sure I was still alive. How could I be?

The lake water surrounding the transparent sides lit up like a giant IMAX theatre and featured a collection of scenes from my life. Either the pyramid or the scenes outside rotated. I couldn't tell which. First, I saw myself sitting by the fire with my father and his strange friends.

Then I watched my life rewind. The different jobs, friends, schools I went to, and my childhood. There were younger versions of my father I barely remembered. My mother; I'd forgotten how beautiful she was. Her image was surreal, not at all like a photograph, but a silent video. She mouthed words and beckoned me.

I never felt so at peace in my life. I wanted to see more, experience more, and know more. I reached out and took my mother's extended hand. I felt her touch, her soft skin. It couldn't be real. We moved through empty space together, like when Superman took Lois for a spin around the world.

My tour was a trip back through my own family history. I saw my grandparents and their grandparents and their great grandparents as we passed through generations.

The movie stopped when a naked couple appeared, the same pair my father had described. I could tell by the woman's genitals and how they looked the same as mine. I wasn't surprised and thought it was the end of the line.

A strange feeling came over me and suggested it wasn't. I locked eyes with my mother. She smiled and was about to lead me on, when I lost my grip on her hand.

Something grabbed my other arm and pulled me in the opposite direction. A firm hand had a grip on my wrist, and I saw a familiar face. My sanctuary had been breached. The feeling of bliss was replaced by sheer terror. I swallowed mouthfuls of water. I felt the pressure change in my inner ears as I was pulled to shallower water. The pyramid got smaller as I was taken further from it.

What's happening to me? Where did my mother go?

Chapter Twenty-One

Trooper Howe grabbed the mic before the dispatcher finished transmitting. His facial expression was like a kid on his first roller coaster ride. Walker found his enthusiasm amusing and tiresome at the same time. Been there and done that so many times, she simply rolled her eyes.

"More lights in the sky Cat, you can't tell me it's all fireworks and Chinese lanterns."

"Or northern lights or low-flying aircraft or spotlights from lake freighters—I've seen it all before, Tom."

"But the caller said air force jets are chasing the strange lights, and you heard the heated discussion back at the marina earlier."

"If there's one thing I've learned from this job, rookie, is just because a citizen says they've seen a UFO, it doesn't mean it's so. Remember the old lady down the beach who couldn't tell a paper kite from an airplane?"

The car engine roared. Howe didn't care what his partner believed any more, there was too much happening. He put the pedal to the metal and activated the flashing red roof light.

"Try to get us there alive, will you partner. You want the siren too?"

"No, it's too hard to hear the dispatcher and whatever else is going on out there."

Walker whistled the Twilight Zone theme and chuckled. Her partner took the next corner practically on two wheels and almost sideswiped an unmarked SUV running with its lights off.

"Who the hell are those idiots?" Trooper Walker yelled out.

Howe managed to stay on the road, narrowly missing the blacked-out vehicle.

"Looks like government tags on that rig."

"Just keep your eyes on the road and I'll worry about the tags. If you put us into that ditch, they might not find us until winter."

They arrived at the scene on the SUV's rear bumper and saw more flashing lights coming down the road. The Captain said he'd meet them there, so Walker waited by the cruiser while Howe ran to the lake behind the cottage.

Two government agents were engaged in an argument with the men he saw earlier, but something else grabbed his attention.

Tom Howe was not a naïve man and thought he'd seen just about everything in life and on the job, but what he saw out in the lake mesmerized and baffled him all at the same time.

The sky and lake appeared black on black, but there was something glowed bright and yellow beneath the surface, as if the sun was about to rise from the water in the middle of the night.

The Trooper approached the lake like a zombie; his gaze fixed on the strange light under water. When he reached the beach one of the men yelled something about his son being out there.

Without a second thought, Howe dropped his gun belt and slipped off his police boots and bullet-proof vest. He heard his partner call out as he hit the water, but he never turned back.

Four

Tom swam towards the light. From the corner of one eye he saw flashing lights and a boat approaching. The water was calm but the Trooper saw bubbles when he neared the submerged object. They made him feel lighter in the water, a welcome relief given the soaked and heavy uniform he was wearing.

He stopped above the bright light and put his face in the water for a better look. He couldn't believe what was below him. The source was a glass triangle-shaped structure, like an underwater greenhouse. The Trooper treaded water for a moment wondering what exactly to do next.

It wasn't like any craft Howe had seen before. He had to know what it was. He took a huge breath and dove below the surface to investigate further. His eyes bulged at the sight. It was like nothing earthly he was aware of.

The sound of an approaching rescue boat grew closer. Tom was halfway down to the object when he saw something even more unbelievable than the triangle itself. There was someone inside it.

The Trooper blinked hard to clear his vision. He was right. There was a man inside the object. It was the younger man from the group by the campfire. Tom's cop instinct kicked in and he went into recovery mode.

He felt duty-bound to rescue the young man from whatever vessel or capsule he was trapped in. It was not only his job, but the right thing to do.

Tom felt the water pressure in his ears and his lungs tingled from the lack of oxygen. The pyramid shaped object looked water-tight and the young man inside appeared to be panicking and waving for help.

Howe had no time to waste, he was out of air. He banged on the glass sides of the triangle, but it was solid with no visible doors or windows.

Tom exhaled a bit of air hoping his lungs would quit screaming. He saw a handprint on one side. Instinct told him to place his own hand there but the imprint was too large and nothing happened. He saw another one on the next side and tried again.

His hand fit perfectly. It slipped right through the glass. He grabbed hold of the young man's arm and pulled. Tom was lightheaded and out of air but held on the best he could. Someone else grabbed the young man by the back of his shirt and pulled him away from Howe and toward the water's surface.

Howe felt himself floating. It was quiet and he saw only black. Thoughts passed through his mind, but he didn't know if he was alive or dead. His body drifted to the bottom and he landed on the strange object. His hand settled back into the imprint. A bright yellow light appeared at the end of a dark tunnel. Tom was at peace.

Four

Chapter Twenty-Two

I coughed up water and wiped it from my eyes. The taste of lake lingered in my mouth and throat. My lungs wheezed. I awoke in a boat full of men in uniform, one repeatedly tried to put an oxygen mask on my face. There were red and white and blue flashing lights nearby and I heard voices on radios. I remembered the yellow light and the pyramid.

There were no other crafts around, and when my eyes searched the water, I saw no signs of my golden triangle. They took me to the city marina. A paramedic checked me over and again tried to force oxygen into my aching lungs. When I refused, he nodded to a military-looking dude dressed in black.

The G-man led me to his car and told me to have a seat in the back. When he asked me why I went into the water, I knew exactly what to say. I told a cute story about how I saw a boat capsize and swam out to try and help. I developed a leg cramp and got sucked under by the current.

The agent looked relieved I didn't try to pass on an alien invasion story. He explained what I actually saw was an unmanned drone that crashed in the lake. It's marker lights resembled the lights on a boat. I played along, nodded and smiled. Dad would have been proud.

All was back to normal when they dropped me off at our cottage. The four men sat quietly in their lawn chairs as I approached the campfire. There was barely a flame to light up their faces. They stared intently at the pile of golden embers as if they wished it were something else.

My father's eyes met mine first. I saw a look of concern, but a hint of something else. The corners of his mouth were curled upwards and I knew what it was. Pride. He stood with open arms and I fell into them. His embrace was warm and secure and offered me the kind of peace I felt inside the pyramid. There was nowhere on earth I'd rather be.

When we parted I turned to greet the others one by one. No words were spoken, only flat smiles and gentle nods of acknowledgement and understanding. I grabbed a couple of logs, put them in the fire and took my chair to complete the circle again.

My dad broke the silence and welcomed me home. The Cambodian said he was glad I made it back. He was looking forward to me cooking breakfast.

The Italian reached in his pocket for a smoke, smiled, and said he wished he had a son to share such a special night. The Spaniard remained quiet and gazed skyward with an expression of loss on his face.

I sat back in my chair and looked up at the heavens. It only took a moment to replay all the events of that night in my mind.

Dropping my head, I scanned the faces of the four men. They shared their wild tales and knew they were blood brothers. I now believed them. I'd been born again and baptized by fire, light, and water and been allowed to join something greater than all of us.

At first there were four. Now we were five.

Chapter Twenty-Three

Trooper Walker was beside herself. They searched for hours and couldn't find Tom Howe's body or any type of vessel that might have sunk in the lake.

Police, rescue boats, and divers worked a grid pattern over and over, expanding it each time to account for the current, but there was no sign of her partner. Only his gun belt, boots and vest, which he'd shed on the beach before entering the lake.

They called him a hero for saving a young man's life. That she was sure of but couldn't believe anything else she'd seen or heard that night.

The government assured everyone it was an air force drone that crashed into the lake. There would be definitive proof once it was recovered. Their theory; Howe's body got tangled in the wreckage and dragged off in the strong current.

That was the official story and the way she was told to write up her incident report. How the media would respond was another story. They eavesdropped on conversations between tight-lipped government agents and State Troopers and would use juicy quotes from hysterical citizens.

Surely there would be skeptics and conspiracy theorists citing another government cover up, but what did it matter? Tom Howe was gone. She knew one of the rescue divers and approached him when he returned to shore for fresh oxygen tanks. He told her there was no trace of her partner, a vessel or aircraft or debris of any kind.

When a G-man glanced his way, he whispered to her. He saw something strange on the lake bottom, a clear impression of a triangle in the sand. The agent walked towards them so the diver stopped talking and returned to his boat.

She turned away from the FIB agent and headed to her cruiser. Images of Tom flashed through her mind. Walker tried to recall earlier conversations with Howe. She couldn't believe he was dead.

Her partner was in great physical shape and an excellent swimmer. Did he really push himself too far and give his own life to save another? What happened to his body? And what the hell was that yellow light she saw in the water where he disappeared? Walker knew there was a better chance of it being a meteorite than a downed drone. She smelled government bullshit.

Trooper Walker drove back to the police detachment by herself. Her captain had offered her a ride home but she said she needed time to process everything. She normally listened to music on the radio but feared the news stations would be blabbing about the loss of her partner and the evening's wild and crazy events.

She stared through the windshield and into the indigo horizon about to give birth to a new sun. Some stars were still visible in the mostly cloudless abyss above. Was there a heaven up there and is that where Tom was? Her eye caught a star that twinkled. She tried to focus on it. A tear ran down her cheek.

Cathy Walker stared at the star that had her attention. It became bigger and brighter than the others and it flashed intermittently, like a signal beacon: - --- --

Four

The End

Author's Note

Although this story is fictional certain parts of it are true. I've visited many of the historical and ancient sites described in this book, and have personally witnessed a strange star-like object changing directions in the sky.

Other events experienced by characters in this story, whether perceived or actual, have been documented by scientists and countless people around the world.

We've all read about government cover-ups and conspiracy theories so I leave it up to you to choose what to believe as fact or fiction. It is my belief that we are not the only form of life that exists in our universe, and that it would be presumptuous to think otherwise.

It's now becoming common practice for people to use natural or organic foods and medicines, and healing procedures. Healers are for real and have been around as long as mankind, but many people still choose to put their faith in religious icons or medical experts who aren't always right.

In the past healer were labelled as magicians, witches or frauds. People are generally afraid of what they don't understand, like techniques and remedies that have been forgotten or shunned over the millennia. Herbal medicines and acupuncture do work. I had a chiropractor pass her hands over my body without touching me, and then perfectly diagnose my aliments and injuries. I'd never met the woman prior to her exam.

Pyramids like the ones in Egypt continue to fascinate us and pose questions that mankind may never answer. Why is it that ancient civilizations possessed certain knowledge and skills that we can't replicate or explain today? How and why did they build similar structures around the world, and what purpose did they really serve?

This story was written to entertain you, but at the same time allow you wonder about the forgotten and unknown...questions that can't be answered but ought to be. And what about the biggest question of all: Are we really alone?

Other Books by Edmond Gagnon

The Norm Strom Crime Series

Rat - Meet the people who risked it all as police informants and visit the criminal netherworld they live in. Take a look into the lives of murderers, drug dealers, prostitutes, and the police who pursue them. Informants may be the scum of the earth, but they could be a family member or neighbor. Police Officer Norm Strom uses his arsenal of informants as secret weapons in his fight against crime.

Bloody Friday - In the aftermath of the Bloody Friday bombings in Belfast Ireland, two best friends set out on different paths in life. One joins the military and later becomes a cop, and the other furthers his involvement with the IRA. Their personal lives and relationships intersect and revolve around drugs and guns and women.

Torch – Arson Detective Norm Strom is always one step behind a serial arsonist who is responsible for burning several buildings in the city's core. He arrests another firebug and recruits him as an informant, hoping to use one torch to extinguish another. The author tells the story in the first and third person, giving the reader a perspective from both the good and the bad.

Finding Hope – Retired Police Detective Norm Strom takes a motorcycle trip from Calgary to Alaska and meets a woman named Hope along the way. She goes missing on the infamous Highway of Tears and Strom lends a hand to the RCMP in their search to find her. The retired cop learns of the hundreds of women who've gone missing and encounters the drug dealers, human traffickers and serial killers who use the Canadian wilderness as their hunting and burial grounds.

Border City Chronicles – Canada and Detroit share more than a river and international border. Murder. This Norm Strom book tells three different stories of homicide, two set in Windsor Ontario and one in Detroit Michigan. Follow one city cop into the underbellies of the motor cities while he investigates the worst of crimes and hunts down the killers responsible.

Edmond Gagnon

And More...

All These Crooked Streets

Crime Fiction

The streets we walk lead to many different places:
> A strip club off the highway during a blizzard.
> A cold case, thirty years unsolved.
> A photographer, in over his head.

Three tales of bad decisions, poor choices and the lure of easy money. The three crime novellas from authors Edmond Gagnon, Christian Laforet and Ben Van Dongen shine a spotlight on the seedy underworld hiding around the corner and in the shadows. It's easy to become lost on *All These Crooked Streets.*

A Casual Traveler

Travel

A collection of short stories and a few poems that chronicle the author's adventures and misadventures around the world. Visit exotic countries in Southeast Asia and Central or South America, and explore great cities like Buenos Aires or Seattle, and ancient sites like Angkor Wat or Machu Picchu.

The author will introduce you to interesting people from around the globe, and share culinary experiences with strange and gourmet foods. Sail on a wooden Junk boat in Ha Long Bay or take an exhilarating motorcycle trip across the country or to the top of Pike's Peak in the Rocky Mountains.

Dare to get off the beaten path and follow Edmond Gagnon to places that you've only dreamed of. Take a trip with *A Casual Traveler.*

Read or buy books online at:

www.edmondgagnon.com

Author Bio

Edmond Gagnon was born and raised in Windsor Ontario, and spent just over thirty-one years as a city police officer, investigating everything from traffic accidents to homicide. He retired an Arson and Fraud Detective.

Upon retiring Ed traveled the world, visiting far away places like Southeast Asia, South America, Belize, and Mexico. He did motorcycle trips from one side of the country to the other, as far north as Alaska and south to Florida.

Ed's story-writing capabilities were conceived on those trips, when he emailed tales of his adventures and misadventures to family and friends. Acting on their suggestions, Ed put all his stories into his first book called *A Casual Traveller*.

Having his musings well received, Ed started his Norm Strom crime fiction series to share his many cop stories. *Rat* was the first book in the series, followed by *Bloody Friday*, *Torch*, *Finding Hope* and *Border City Chronicles*. He also collaborated with local authors Ben Van Dongen and Christian Laforet in the crime anthology *All These Crooked Streets*.

Ed continues to travel the world with his wife Cathryn. Visiting special places far and near is what piqued Ed's interest in the paranormal, and inspired him to write this thriller called, *Four*. Be sure to check out his website and blog for book updates, trip stories, and reviews on books, movies, and restaurants.

All of Edmond Gagnon's Books can be read or purchased online at:
www.edmondgagnon.com

CPSIA information can be obtained
at www.ICGtesting.com
Printed in the USA
LVHW031951151019
634329LV00002B/2/P